CHOSEN MATE

A CRESCENT MOON STORY

Katie Reus

Copyright © 2019 by Katie Reus

All rights reserved. Except as permitted under the U.S. Copyright Act of 1976, no part of this publication may be reproduced, distributed, or transmitted in any form or by any means, or stored in a database or retrieval system, without the prior written permission of the author. Thank you for buying an authorized version of this book and complying with copyright laws. You're supporting writers and encouraging creativity.

Cover art: Jaycee of Sweet 'N Spicy Designs
Author website: www.katiereus.com

Publisher's Note: This is a work of fiction. Names, characters, places, and incidents are either the products of the author's imagination or used fictitiously, and any resemblance to actual persons, living or dead, or business establishments, organizations or locales is completely coincidental.

Chosen Mate/Katie Reus -- 1st ed.

ISBN-13: 978-1-63556-137-1
ISBN-10: 1-63556-137-X

eISBN-13: 9781635561364

Praise for the novels of Katie Reus

"...a wild hot ride for readers. The story grabs you and doesn't let go." —*New York Times* bestselling author, Cynthia Eden

"Has all the right ingredients: a hot couple, evil villains, and a killer action-filled plot.... [The] Moon Shifter series is what I call Grade-A entertainment!"
—Joyfully Reviewed

"I could not put this book down.... Let me be clear that I am not saying that this was a good book *for* a paranormal genre; it was an excellent romance read, *period*." —All About Romance

"Reus strikes just the right balance of steamy sexual tension and nail-biting action....This romantic thriller reliably hits every note that fans of the genre will expect." —*Publishers Weekly*

"Prepare yourself for the start of a great new series!... I'm excited about reading more about this great group of characters."
—Fresh Fiction

"A sexy, well-crafted paranormal romance that succeeds with smart characters and creative world building."
—Kirkus Reviews

Continued...

"You'll fall in love with Katie's heroes."
—*New York Times* bestselling author, Kaylea Cross

"Both romantic and suspenseful, a fast-paced sexy book full of high stakes action." —Heroes and Heartbreakers

"Nonstop action, a solid plot, good pacing, and riveting suspense."
—RT Book Reviews

"Sexy military romantic suspense." —USA Today

"Enough sexual tension to set the pages on fire."
—*New York Times* bestselling author, Alexandra Ivy

"*Avenger's Heat* hits the ground running... This is a story of strength, of partnership and healing, and it does it brilliantly."
—Vampire Book Club

"*Mating Instinct* was a great read with complex characters, serious political issues and a world I am looking forward to coming back to." —All Things Urban Fantasy

CHAPTER ONE

Malcolm knocked on Leslie's door, steeling himself to see the sweet, strong she-wolf.

As always.

She'd joined his pack a year and a half ago after escaping an abusive ex—who was now dead, thanks to his pack—and she'd almost completely come out of her shell since then. At least with him. A lot of that had to do with him being alpha of the Kendrick pack, but he'd loved seeing her blossom into the funny, outgoing female she was.

He wanted her more than he'd ever wanted anything in his entire long life. But as the alpha, he was in a position of power, and he never wanted her to feel obligated or as if she owed him anything. It put him in an impossible situation, as every dominant part of him wanted to make a move. But... he simply couldn't. Not yet.

Her smile was wide as she greeted him, revealing twin dimples in her cheeks. Her light brown skin was practically glowing as she stepped back. "Thank you so much for coming by." Now that summer was slowly creeping in, she had on shorts that showed off lean, muscular legs and a flimsy little yellow tank top that hugged her full breasts in a way that made him jealous of the shirt.

Digging deep, he kept his wolf in check as he leaned in and kissed the top of her head. As if he was simply the caring alpha who'd stopped by to help out a packmate. Which he was, but she was more than a packmate. He subtly inhaled her scent, but shut down what it did to him. He had to for his sanity. "No problem. So what exactly is going on with your sink?"

"I must have the worst luck in the world when it comes to anything mechanical. The faucet isn't working again and it's leaking a bit under the sink. Nothing terrible, but this is the third time it's happened." She playfully poked him in the shoulder with a manicured fingernail. "I'm starting to think that someone's work isn't up to par." She snickered, since he was the one who'd fixed her sink last time.

He liked how relaxed she was with him, because even six months ago she wouldn't have joked around about his alleged shoddy workmanship.

Though he knew it wasn't shoddy. No, more likely, one of his packmates had loosened one of the washers again to get him over here. Nosy, matchmaking wolves were trying to push him and Leslie together, and he was pretty sure his brother—who was also the second-in-command—had taken a hand in all this. Sneaky wolf.

"Yeah, I need to talk with that slacker." He glanced around as he stepped inside, looking for Elijah, her thirteen-month-old son. "Where's my favorite pup?" Normally Elijah would have rushed him, toddling at him like a drunken sailor before launching himself into Malcolm's arms. He had a soft spot for all pups but with Elijah, the little guy had stolen his heart.

Just like Leslie had.

"With my mom, getting spoiled. Where else?" Leslie's smile was easy and sweet.

And he felt that smile like a punch to his gut.

See me, his wolf practically shouted, and he felt nothing like the 200-plus-year-old alpha wolf he was. Under any other circumstances, his wolf would have already staked a claim and let his chosen mate know that he was courting her and that they were meant to be together.

Leslie had been through a lot, though. She'd dealt with something no she-wolf—hell, no one—should ever have to deal with.

An abusive mate.

The idea was repugnant to Malcolm. Mates were supposed to treasure and protect their significant others. That was simply the way it was in the shifter world. They were different than humans in that there was very little domestic abuse.

Most wolves, or shifters in general, wouldn't put up with that shit. Him least of all. If her ex hadn't already been dead, Malcolm would have taken him out personally.

He adjusted his toolbelt as he strode into the kitchen with her. "Something smells delicious," he said, eyeing the basket on top of the white and gray-veined quartz countertop.

"Ursula dropped off a bunch of baked goods. You hungry?"

Technically he was hungry, but not for food. He willed his dick to stay right where it was, however, because there was no way he could hide a hard on once he stretched out under her sink on his back. He cleared his throat. "I'm good, but thanks. Oh, I brought you these," he said off-handedly. From one of the pockets of his tool belt, he pulled out a little plastic bag full of the triple-dipped chocolate cashew clusters that he'd special-ordered for her.

Her eyes widened as she held them to her chest. "Thank you! I'll have to hide them from... *everyone* who stops by."

"That's probably wise." He watched her expression of pure happiness as she held the gift close and he really, really wondered what had been wrong with her dead mate. She was pure joy and sunshine and her ex had wanted to hide her away, to snuff out her bright light by controlling her and breaking her down. Thankfully he hadn't succeeded.

She side-stepped a couple of the cleaning supply bottles she'd spread out on the floor and hid the bag above the refrigerator in a little tin, making him smile.

Since she'd already emptied out the space under the cabinets and had laid out a towel and bucket underneath, he quickly crouched down. If he found out who had done this, he was going to kick their ass. Well-meaning interference or not, Leslie didn't deserve to deal with this kind of hassle.

As he got on his back and slid in, she started moving around the kitchen, her wild lavender scent teasing him, driving him crazy. It made him think of the forest, of running free at night under a full moon—with her by his side.

"So a human from town asked me out on a date," she said conversationally and casual as anything.

He jerked upward, banging his head on the curved pipe above him. Somehow he reined in a curse as he heard her opening the refrigerator door. "Ah, what?" Maybe he'd misheard.

"Yeah, just yesterday. A nice enough random human from town. He was at the diner at the same time I was. I've seen him around and he seems decent." Her tone wasn't overly enthusiastic, which was something.

"What human?" There, that sounded normal enough, even though he was gritting his teeth, imagining punching whoever had asked her out. No one in the pack would dare ask her out. Even if no one had outright called him out on his feelings for her, everyone knew. It was in the subtle way he acted around her and they'd all picked up on it. Well, his brother called him out on it, but he was the only one brave enough.

"Ah, Marcus something. He owns the auto body shop. You know, he's got a bunch of tattoos."

He did know, and the guy was a good-looking bastard. Malcolm had actually admired the guy's body art, had wondered where he'd gotten his ink done. Now he just wanted to take the guy's head off. Which, yes, was barbaric and savage. But he was a wolf, not a human. Not that humans were very civilized anyway. "What'd you tell him?"

He listened to her moving around, heard her pouring coffee then sitting at the table. She let out a little sigh. "I said I didn't know and took his phone number."

Some of the tension inside him eased. "So... you're ready to start dating again?" That was definitely news to him. If she was moving on, he wanted her to move on with him. Forever.

"I guess. I just..." She trailed off again as he tightened the washer.

The fix was simple enough—but the loosening had definitely been intentional. Even though he was done, he remained where he was, clanging around and making noises so she would keep talking. He'd noticed that she always felt comfortable talking and opening up to him whenever he was working on something. But if he got out from under the cabinet and they made eye contact, she would close up. He knew that well enough from experience. "What?" he gently pushed.

"I don't know that I'm ready to date, but I am ready for physical touch again. I'm starting to feel agitated, edgy lately. My wolf needs touch, you know?" He could hear her fingernail tapping against her coffee mug.

He bit back a growl. The thought of anyone touching her but him had all his claws begging for release, his wolf desperate to be free so he could run and run and run all of this rage off. He didn't even trust himself to spar with anyone. If he did, he was likely to accidentally hurt a packmate. "Physical touch?" Somehow he forced the words out—because physical touch was simply code for sex. She was ready for *sex*.

"You know what it's like. Wolves need touch. And... it's been a while for me. Even well before Elijah was born. And if I'm being honest, I want to be sure I can have normal sex again. Especially after..." She swallowed hard.

Her ex had abused her, and Malcolm knew that he'd raped her more than once. When she'd first come to live with his pack, her mother, Luna, had told him about the abuse she'd endured. And that thought killed any sensual ideas about her that he might have been entertaining at the moment. Not for the first time Malcolm wished her mate was alive so he could kill the bastard all over again. He just wished he'd been the one to kill him in the first place.

"So why a human?" His wolf slashed at him, telling him to stop asking stupid questions and to demand to know why she wanted anyone other than him. Hell, if the circumstances had been different, if she hadn't come to his pack traumatized, he'd have already let her know how he felt, would have made a much bolder move. And right now, when she was telling him she was ready for sex, he would have gladly offered to let her use him. Over and over.

As much as she wanted.

"Humans are safer than supernaturals. I would be in control the whole time."

"Why couldn't you be in control with a wolf?" Both he and his wolf side wanted this answer. He was dominant by nature but he would give up all of his control for Leslie. At least until she felt safe with him. He couldn't change who he was, but he could adapt, could be what she needed.

"I don't know, I guess I just feel like, in the back of my mind it may be easier with a human."

Malcolm was done fixing the pipe and this was about all he could hear about her having sex with someone else. Even if it was just hypothetical.

He'd been trying to court her for the last six months, slowly and subtly. Hell, he'd wanted her since he'd met her, since she'd shown up here pregnant and in need of shelter a year and a half ago. But that had been way too soon. Only in the last six months had he noticed a shift in her. Obviously he'd been far too subtle or she wouldn't be talking with him about dating someone else. He knew Leslie would never, ever try to hurt him. She was too soft-hearted to knowingly hurt *anyone.*

"Well, I'm sure if you went for a wolf instead of a human, someone from the pack would be more than happy to satisfy all your needs." And by someone, he meant *himself.* Because yeah, he'd take off the head of a wolf who touched her too. He slid out from under the countertop and watched her, wanting to see her reaction.

She stared at him for a long moment, before clearing her throat and looking down at her mug. "Yeah, maybe," she muttered. "But then things would be awkward afterward."

"Maybe not." Shifting slightly, he started putting all of her cleaning supplies back where they belonged, tamping down the urge to go to her right now and kiss away any thoughts of her with someone else out of her gorgeous head.

"No maybe about it. I'm not looking for a mate, and you know how wolves can be... Hey, stop doing that." She knelt down next to him and swatted at him. "You're the alpha."

"Exactly. I take care of my packmates."

Something shifted in her gaze, almost like disappointment, but it was there so quickly and then gone that he wasn't sure what he'd seen. Wasn't sure what to make of it at all.

The only thing he knew was that he was completely and utterly smitten with Leslie, and he wanted nothing more than to satisfy all of her emotional and physical needs.

That was *very* high on his priority list. He wanted to taste between her legs as she came, wanted to hear her calling out his name as she dug her fingernails into his scalp. Wanted her so happy and sated from climaxing so many damn times, that she wore his scent for everyone to know she was claimed.

Now that he knew she was ready to move on, he was going to be right there for her.

CHAPTER TWO

Well, that had gone well. Leslie lay her forehead against the closed front door after Malcolm had left, feeling sorry for herself. She wasn't sure why she'd started to tell the object of her fantasies that she was thinking about dating.

Okay, that was a big fat *lie*. She knew exactly why she'd told him. They were friends and he was easy to talk to, sure, but truthfully, she'd been hoping for some sort of reaction. To see if he even cared if she started dating. *Something.*

But she'd gotten exactly nothing.

Which was the answer to the unasked question that she'd needed. Even though it cut deep. She'd been drawn to Malcolm from the moment she'd arrived on his land. Even as messed up as she'd been back then, her wolf half had felt safe around him. And that was saying something. She hadn't been remotely ready for any kind of relationship, not with her being pregnant and trying to settle into a new pack, a new life—and starting to feel safe again.

But the last year they'd been working together, since she was now the pack's accountant, and she'd started to sort of obsess over him. Or maybe that was the wrong word, but he consumed her thoughts and she had all sorts of sexy, naked fantasies about him.

So yeah, okay, obsess worked.

But she must have built up an attraction between them in her mind. After the very poor choices she'd made in her first mate—an abusive monster—why on earth would she think that she was good enough for the alpha of the pack? God, she was such a fool. Sure, he came over and helped out with things when she needed it, but as he'd so clearly stated moments ago, he took care of all his packmates.

Because that was his job. One he'd taken on willingly, sure, but it was still his responsibility. Which meant she was his responsibility as part of the pack. Not a female he wanted to get intimate with.

The sexy male was laid-back and sweet, but he was definitely an alpha. So if he was into her, he would've gotten all growly and possessive the moment she'd mentioned dating someone else. She imagined that his very faint Scottish accent would have gotten a bit thicker too—because she'd noticed that when something agitated him, that accent slipped through. It had been a century since he'd lived in Scotland but very occasionally—when he was really pissed—it got stronger. And she loved it.

The only silver lining of all this was now she was glad she'd told him, glad that she hadn't outright embarrassed herself by letting him know her feelings for him. Which were clearly one-sided. She could just imagine how embarrassing it would have been because he would have tried to let her down easy. She winced at the thought.

Taking a few deep breaths, she grabbed her cell phone and called that human male. But after she talked to the human who'd asked her out on a date—telling him that yes, she would have lunch with him tomorrow—she wasn't sure how she felt. Not better, that was for sure. Just... ugh. Sort of untethered and lost in general.

But she needed to get out there again, to stop hiding away from the world.

Since coming to live with the Kendrick pack, she hadn't been hiding exactly, but it had taken her a while to come out of her shell again, to feel alive again. After being mated to Jude, she'd felt like a shadow of her former self. All hollowed out and pathetic because he'd certainly pulled the wool over her eyes.

Before they'd mated, he'd been wonderful and sweet and nothing at all like the man who'd started hitting her, telling her that she didn't need to work outside the home because she needed to take care of him. The man who'd been demanding of all her time and energy to the point where it had been easier to just quit her job than argue with him all the time. She hadn't realized at first that was exactly what he'd wanted. She'd fallen right into his trap.

And if he hadn't threatened her mother—and if Leslie hadn't been absolutely certain he would have followed through on that threat—she would have left him long before the six-month mark of their mating. As a rule, she-wolves didn't put up with shit from anyone.

But he'd had brothers, and she and her mother had been no match for them in physical strength. He'd made it almost impossible for her to be alone with her mom, let alone escape their pack's territory. And if she hadn't been smart about it, hadn't asked for outside help from her aunt Sapphire, Leslie knew without a doubt that she and her mom would be dead. Strong she-wolves or not, going up against a bunch of violent male wolves was tough.

Leslie shook those thoughts off and pulled open the front door, breathing in the fresh mountain air. Summer was right around the corner, spring fading into the distance already. Even if there was a chilly breeze rolling through, she didn't care. Her body ran hotter than humans' and the feel of all the fresh air and sunlight on her arms and legs was wonderful.

Slipping on her flip-flops, she hurried down the stairs of her cabin's front porch and walked right next door to find her mom and her son playing on that front porch. Elijah was in his wolf form, tumbling around and doing actual somersaults. Though he kept landing on his belly, his paws splayed out since he wasn't remotely in control of himself yet. His antics were definitely the cutest thing she had ever seen in her life.

"Did Malcolm fix your sink?" her mom, Luna, asked from her position on the porch, where she sat cross-legged in shorts and a T-shirt, her dark hair in little braids down her back.

"Yep." She leaned against the porch column, watching her son race back and forth along the porch. "He seems to have extra energy this morning." That was saying something, considering the type of energy and metabolism that shifters had as a whole. But he was a pup and they were always ready to go. Thankfully he slept well at night.

Her mom's dark eyes sparkled. "He's just like you were at that age."

She grinned because she'd definitely been a handful. "I was thinking of heading into town today and getting my hair done." It was Sunday and the pack's salon was open, whereas they wouldn't be tomorrow. She'd learned since moving here that pack businesses in town tended to close on Mondays so everyone got a break. And thanks to the tourists who frequented their mountain town, they saw most of their business on weekends anyway. Her job was different, since she worked on the pack's property and she made her own hours.

"Go on. I've got this little furball." Her mom opened her arms as Elijah jumped into them. Then just as quickly, he shifted into a little boy, the change so seamless, the spark of magic bursting and then fading as he snuggled up in his nana's arms before falling into a light sleep.

She missed being able to fall asleep like that. Now at nights she often stared at the ceiling, begging for rest that rarely came—because she had an itch she couldn't scratch. Only one wolf could do that. But she wasn't going to get all caught up in her head right now.

"Thanks, Mama," she said, bending down and kissing her mom on the forehead, then her son on his cheek. "I'm probably going to get a manicure too, but call me if you need me."

"Take your time. And definitely get the manicure. Your nails are starting to get sad."

"Hey!" Then she looked down and winced because it was true. She had gel nail polish but they'd grown out so far it looked ridiculous.

But she'd been so busy at work lately that she hadn't had time to get away. "Yeah, you're right. By the way, I have a date tomorrow afternoon." She tossed the news out all casual even though she felt anything but casual about the date. She'd decided to do it on her lunch break because then she would have the perfect excuse to leave if things got uncomfortable.

Her mom's eyebrows raised in true surprise. "A date? With Malcolm?"

"No! And hush," she said, looking around. She didn't want anyone in the pack thinking she had set her sights on Malcolm. The mere thought was ridiculous. "A human in town asked me out. I figured it can't hurt to see what's out there."

Her mom simply made a humming sound as she stood, cradling a still-snoozing Elijah in her arms.

"What?" she asked.

"I didn't say anything."

Leslie narrowed her gaze. "You didn't need to."

"I have nothing to say on the matter. You are a grown she-wolf and I'm glad you're getting out there again. It's time." Truth rolled off her mom in waves, easing the weird tension inside Leslie. "Now go take care of yourself."

Feeling much lighter, she hurried down the short set of stairs. She might even get a pedicure today too. And she wasn't doing it because she was going on a date tomorrow. She was doing this for her.

Her ex had been so critical of her anytime she'd gone to the salon, demanding to know who she was getting "all prettied up for". His dumbass words, not hers.

So she'd finally just stopped going. In hindsight, she realized just how controlling he'd started to be even at the beginning of their mating. He really hadn't hidden who he was for very long after they'd mated. Maybe if she'd insisted on a longer courting period, she'd have seen him for who he was. Instead, she'd been foolish enough to jump into a mating without getting to know him well. But she'd been attracted and she'd believed in the whole fairytale thing even if she'd never felt the mating pull with him.

She'd convinced herself that the mating pull was just something that had been built up by other wolves. In reality, she'd so desperately wanted what her parents had—before her dad died. She'd only been two at the time, but the way her mom still talked about her dad made it clear that they'd had a once-in-a-lifetime type of mating.

Well that fairytale happily ever after hadn't existed for Leslie. And she had to stop believing in foolish dreams.

CHAPTER THREE

Malcolm leaned back in his chair, stretching his legs out as his younger brother jumped up onto his desk, scattering papers like some crazed pup. "What the hell is wrong with you?"

"Nothing. Just came to bug you." Hudson's grin grew as he knocked a couple papers off the desk with a finger, just to get a rise out of Malcolm.

"No respect," he muttered. If it had been anyone else in the pack, he wouldn't have put up with this, but Hudson was his younger brother and there were different rules for the two of them. Right now it was clear that Hudson was in "annoying little brother mode" and not mature second-in-command. It didn't matter that Hudson was over two hundred years old, some days he acted no better than a pup. "So where's your better half? And why aren't you with her?" Malcolm asked dryly. He had a shit ton of paperwork to catch up on, and then he planned to go running in wolf form. He was still off kilter after that talk with Leslie yesterday. Even the thought of her letting some male touch her had his wolf edgy.

"She's out running with the boys."

The boys were Hudson's young twin pups. The two of them got into all sorts of mischief and couldn't seem to keep their clothes on. Whenever he saw them, they were naked or in wolf form. He knew once they hit four or so, they'd grow out of this phase.

"So... did you stop by for something? Or are you just here to bug me?" Leaning down, he started picking up some of the scattered papers.

"Just wanted to see what you're up to for lunch today." Hudson had a cat-that-ate-the-canary grin and a glint in his eyes Malcolm recognized.

His brother was up to something. He stood and crossed his arms over his chest. "Nothing. Why?"

"Just wanted to see if you could join me, Erica and the boys for lunch." Now his expression went carefully neutral.

Oh yeah, he was up to something. "Sounds good. I'll be free in an hour." His office was on pack land—in one of the cabins—so it was a quick walk across their compound. Compound meaning the big spread of cabins out in the Montana wilderness. Though not as wild as it used to be since they were fairly close to town. They owned thousands of acres with plenty of room to run, free of human eyes. "Until then, some of us actually have to work," he said dryly.

Hudson jumped off the desk, his boots making a soft thud against the oversized throw rug. "I'll clear out. By the way, what's Leslie doing for lunch today?"

Malcolm shifted slightly, narrowing his gaze at his brother. "Why do I get the feeling you already know the answer to that?"

"She was at the salon yesterday getting her hair done. Nails too. Erica told me she looks fantastic."

Leslie always looked sexy, and she didn't need her nails or hair or anything else done for that. She was a natural beauty, inside and out. "Can you get to the damn point?"

His brother took a step back from the desk, inching closer to the door. "I can't help but wonder if she got all that done for the date she's going on during lunch today." He looked at his watch. "I bet she's leaving soon too."

"Date?" Malcolm rounded the desk, shoving his chair out of the way before he even realized he'd moved.

But Hudson was long gone, his cackling laughter echoing in his wake as he practically sprinted from the cabin.

Yesterday Leslie had told him she was maybe thinking about dating but she was actually going out with someone? Not bothering to subdue his growl, he stalked out of his office, his brother long gone by the time he stomped out the front door. His office was part of his home, but it was sectioned off and separate so when he was in there, people knew he was working.

Leslie was in one of the other pack office buildings—right next to his home. It was a cabin too, but they'd set it up with offices instead of bedrooms. As he approached the other building, he was surprised to find her outside and shutting the door behind her.

She jumped when she saw him, and he wasn't sure if it was because he'd surprised her or if it was one of those delayed reactions from the abuse she'd suffered.

"Hey, Malcolm." She slid her crossbody bag over her head as she descended the stairs. She had indeed gotten her hair done, her dark curls straightened into soft waves, and her nails were a sparkly purple instead of blue today.

"Hey, just coming by to see if you wanted to grab lunch." And to see if she was going on a date.

She cleared her throat. "I can't. I've got plans."

"Oh? Lunch with your mom?" He definitely wanted an answer.

"No," she said, tossing her hair over her shoulder almost nervously. "I decided to go out with that human. The one who asked me out. Figured it can't hurt."

He ground his molars, but forced out a smile. Barely. "Right, well, have fun." He turned away then, because he knew if he stayed a second longer, he was going to say something he would regret. And of all the people he'd ever known in his entire two-hundred plus years, he never wanted to say something he regretted to Leslie. It would rip his heart out to hurt her. She was all softness and sunshine, and he couldn't stand the thought of her frowning or hurt because of him.

He also couldn't stand the thought of her out with another male. Yep, if she was moving on, he needed to make damn sure she moved with him.

CHAPTER FOUR

Leslie sat across from Marcus and couldn't help but think that he was more or less an alternate version of Malcolm. Which was pretty much the entire reason she'd said yes to the date. His name even started with an M. He was human, yes, but he had tattoos, dark hair, blue eyes and a nice smile. Just like Malcolm. Though their tattoos weren't anything alike, even if they both had sleeves. And when he talked, he was sincere and kind but… There was absolutely no attraction. He was funny though, and she appreciated that. But as far as that intangible thing that got her heart racing, her blood pumping and her fantasies going into overtime? Nope.

Not even a sliver of it now.

"So is your son's father in the picture?" he asked casually as he sat back, pushing his empty plate slightly in front of him.

"No." Her abusive asshole of a mate was dead but she didn't want him to feel sorry for her because she was a widow. Because she was actually glad her former mate was gone. "It's just me and my little guy. Well, that's not true because I've got my mom and… friends and family." She stumbled on the last two words because she couldn't very well say pack. He wouldn't know what she was talking about. Which was another reason she shouldn't have come out with him. Shifters and humans very rarely dated. Because if they ever got serious, the shifter had to tell the human about their other nature—and they had to be very sure that the human would be able to deal with it.

"That's good then. I was raised by a single mom and a bunch of aunts. I think I turned out all right." He lifted a shoulder, giving her a self-deprecating smile.

She laughed lightly. "I would say so. Look, lunch has been great, but…"

"I already know there's not going to be another date. There's no chemistry here."

She blinked at his bluntness. "You're so hot, I wish there was," she blurted, then felt herself flush. What the hell was wrong with her?

Apparently she'd lost her filter today. Seeing Malcolm earlier, having him not seem to care *at all* about her going on a date, had knocked her off balance in the worst way possible. She was busy pining after him and he was clearly not pining after her. Sure, they went to lunch all the time, but that was just packmates going out as friends. Man, she would be so embarrassed if Malcolm could read her thoughts. Luckily she'd been able to hide her attraction to him, but she wondered how long she'd be able to.

Marcus let out a startled laugh. "Likewise. I wish there was as well." He let out a sigh, and there was something sad in his expression she could read only because she felt it herself.

"Is there someone else you're into?" she asked quietly.

"Yeah. Someone I'm trying to get over. You kinda look like her," he muttered, as if embarrassed.

Oh wow, she was right there with him. Apparently they were riding the same wavelength of pathetic-ness. "I completely relate. I'm currently trying to get over a crush that's not reciprocated." Crush felt like far too juvenile a word for what she felt for Malcolm, but she wasn't going to tell this guy that she needed to get over her obsession. *That wouldn't make her sound pathetic or desperate at all.*

"Hopefully we can still be friends though?"

"I would like that." And she meant it. It was always tricky being friends with humans, but she'd managed it over the years. Of course, she was only in her thirties, unlike many others in the pack, some of whom were over two hundred years old—including Malcolm.

Dammit, she had to stop thinking about him. But he just seemed to pop up in her every waking thought. And her dreams. Gah, she couldn't get the male out of her head.

They each paid for their lunch, though Marcus tried to pay for hers since he'd invited her. But she didn't want to start off their friendship that way. She could tell it bothered him to let her pay, which made him that much more adorable. Still, he paled in comparison to Malcolm.

Everyone did.

By the time she made it back to the pack's land, she was surprised to find Malcolm sitting on the front steps of her office cabin. Cross-legged, he was leaning back and working on his laptop, but he stopped as she approached.

"Hey, everything okay?" She sat on the steps a few feet away from him, stretching her legs out under the sunlight. It was warm on her skin and made her wish she was out running in wolf form. Mainly because being near Malcolm put her on edge, had her whole body waking up with an awareness she wished she could ignore.

He set his laptop aside and watched her so intently with those bright blue eyes that she resisted the urge to squirm. "How was your date?"

She frowned. "Ah, fine. Is everything okay with work?"

He paused for a long moment. "Yeah. I'm headed to The Golden Grape Vineyard and Winery. It's not on the market officially, but it's going up for sale and I'm thinking about buying it as an investment for the pack. I was hoping you could take time off and come with me. You can look at all the numbers on the way there."

"Of course I'll go." He was the alpha so if he asked for something, she was going to do it. She would do *anything* he asked, she thought, her mind straying to completely nonwork things. Quickly she shook those thoughts off so her body wouldn't react. Because he would scent it, and then she would simply die of embarrassment. Yep, she would cut a hole in the ground and let it swallow her up. "I want to go spend some time with Elijah first. He's been with my mom all morning. Do we need to leave right now?"

"No. We can head out in an hour. Go give him cuddles."

That was one of the nice things about being part of a good pack. They all worked as a unit and family was always going to come first. So she never felt guilty about taking time off during the day to spend time with her son.

Soon she'd be alone in a vehicle with Malcolm. The thought was exciting and... nerve-wracking. That non-date had just driven home exactly how perfect Malcolm was. Unfortunately, she didn't think he would ever see her as anything other than a packmate.

* * *

"So what do you think of the numbers?" Malcolm asked Leslie, though he was pretty sure he knew what her opinion would be. He'd already run them himself—he just wanted an excuse to spend time with her.

She looked up from the tablet and glanced out the car window at the beautiful passing scenery. Fresh flowers and bright greenery covered the fields and mountainside, the explosion of color welcome after the long winter.

When she looked at him, her expression was thoughtful. "They look good. They could be better, but it looks as if there was a shift or something six months ago and they stopped making as much of a profit. I can't figure out why, though. Their online sales are fine and none of their vendors changed and nothing else discernible changed, but the sales directly at the winery's retail shop have plummeted so it's got to be something internal with their employees."

"The owners are going through a divorce and everything hit six months ago. A few of their staff have quit over all the volatility."

"That makes sense then. If you're going to invest, I say scoop it up now. Before it gets even worse. Will you have packmates run it or leave humans in charge?"

"Maybe both. Probably both." His pack didn't know anything about running a winery and from what he could tell, they had very qualified humans running the place. It was the couple who owned it who had completely lost control and their finances were starting to suffer because of it.

She nodded thoughtfully. "For purely selfish reasons, I'm glad you asked me to go today. I've been wanting to check out some of the local wineries, this one included."

He knew that. She'd mentioned it more than once, and he hadn't actually needed her to come with him today. He just wanted time alone with her so he could make it clear that he was interested.

"So tell me about your date." He kept his voice casual even though his claws were ready to extend and rip into the steering wheel. He needed to know what he was up against.

She shifted against her seat. "We decided to be friends."

He let out a snort. That male had made the right choice in walking away. Though the human was a fool if he just wanted to be friends with her. While Malcolm did treasure her friendship, he wanted more. So much more that he could barely contain his wolf sometimes. Every night when he closed his eyes, he saw her, thought about her... fantasized about her.

She shot him a frown. "Why is that funny?"

"You're holding back on me."

"And you're being exceptionally nosy today." She sniffed slightly and looked out the window.

He lifted a shoulder, feigning a casualness he didn't feel. "I haven't gotten any good intel in a while."

She laughed at that. "I think you mean gossip."

"Same thing." Wolves were the worst gossips, males or females. It didn't matter. They were always up in each other's business and he could admit that he kept a pulse on his entire pack. It was easy when shifters liked to share so much damn information about each other. Sometimes too much.

"Fine," she said, sighing. "He was perfectly nice, funny, attractive, but there was no attraction for either of us."

"Then he's a moron," Malcolm muttered.

She whipped around to look at him. "What?"

"You're stunning. He's an idiot."

Her scent shifted ever so slightly and for a moment he thought she might say something but at the last minute she murmured, "Nah. He's just trying to get over someone and thought going out with me would help."

Whatever, the guy was a fool, but that was good for Malcolm. He was done waiting.

Leslie cleared her throat. "So, are you dating? Because turnabout is fair play, Mr. Nosy."

He made a sort of strangled sound. "No."

Now she was the one who snorted.

"What?"

"It's just hard to believe." She glanced at him for a second before turning to look back out the window. More flashes of color bloomed as they drove into slightly flatter territory.

"Trust me, if I was dating someone you would know with the way our pack gossips."

That got a light laugh out of her but she didn't respond. Or look back at him. And he couldn't get a read on her scent. It was too muddled.

"I'm not looking to date or fuck anyway. I'm looking for a mate." He needed to lay it out. He wasn't going to make her feel uncomfortable or get in her face when they were on a car ride and she had nowhere to go, but he might as well be honest about this. Because it was important that she understood where he was in life. What he wanted—her.

She shifted in her seat slightly. "Really?"

"Yes, really. I'm over two-hundred years old. I don't date. And if I'm being honest, I've been ready for a while." Even before he'd met Leslie, his wolf had grown far too dissatisfied with just sex. He wanted to mate, and for wolves that meant for life. Usually. Unless the mating turned out to be an absolute disaster, but again that was fairly rare for their kind. No, he wanted a partner, someone to have his back and vice versa. Being the alpha got lonely sometimes, but whenever he was with Leslie, something deep inside him felt at peace.

She made a sort of humming sound and then spoke, her voice strained. "Well, any female would be lucky to have you."

He froze for a moment at the strain in her voice. He wasn't sure what it meant, but he would find out. At least now she knew that he wasn't looking for a quick fuck. And damn he was tired of these baby steps, but she was worth it. He needed to change the subject though, to put her back on steadier footing. "Since we're headed to the winery, what's your favorite wine?"

She seemed startled by the change in subject, but smiled. "I'm not sure about their brands, but in general, for red, I prefer pinot noir and for white, pinot grigio. But it kind of depends on what I'm eating too. Oh, and I love champagne regardless of food. I feel like you can't go wrong with it. It's bubbly and light and makes me feel like I'm celebrating something when I drink it."

He smiled at her description. "Well I think since we're going to be touring this place, we'll have to do a tasting. A very in-depth one."

"Is that right?"

"Of course. For research purposes only. I am a serious alpha and this is serious work."

She laughed, the sound unrestrained and throaty, her amusement wrapping around him in a tight embrace. Damn, but he wanted to spend the rest of his life making her laugh like that.

"Well, if it's in the name of research, I am totally here for this. I feel a little guilty to be out of work though."

"Why should you feel guilty? You deserve to enjoy your life." The words came out far harsher than he'd intended them and they weren't directed at her. He knew where the "guilt" was coming from. Her stupid dead ex had put that there.

Luckily, she didn't seem to shrink into herself. If she had, he wouldn't have been able to stand it. Instead, she shoved out a sigh. "I know. I was so full of life before... Just *before* everything. And now that I'm getting back to normal, I have to remind myself that it's absolutely okay to take time for me even if it takes me away from Elijah. Though I do feel a little guilty leaving him sometimes. And that has nothing to do with my ex."

"That pup is surrounded by love 24/7 and he knows it."

"I know. I guess there's just a small part of me that's terrified he'll somehow get taken away. I know Jude and his brothers are dead, but... that fear still lingers inside me."

His wolf prowled inside him, restless and edgy at the thought of anyone looking to threaten her or her son. "If anyone tried to take him away from you, I would kill them." His tone was far more savage than it should have been, even if the words were true.

To his surprise, she gave him a startled smile. "That's good to hear. No one would stand a chance against you."

Her simple words of praise did something to his wolf. He felt like a freaking peacock wanting to preen under the warmth of her faith in him. Instead, he grunted and looked back at the road.

Slowly, he could see the walls she'd built up coming down. Slowly but surely.

Good, because he wasn't going to stop until he pulled them all down.

CHAPTER FIVE

"Okay, this is incredible," Leslie said as they sat down at the little table on the veranda outside the Mediterranean-style winery.

Malcolm had asked the staff to set this up for them so he and Leslie could relax. He'd already put in an offer even before this trip so they were eager to do anything he asked. Now that he knew she was dating, it was on. And he wasn't above being a sneaky wolf when it came to claiming her heart.

They'd spent an hour and a half touring the place and looking at the vineyard plantation and the winery itself. Through his research, he'd learned that some nearby places were simple vineyards and they sold their grapes to outside wineries, but this place functioned as both and was a licensed winery. Which was good for his business intentions. Now, however, he wanted her to relax and kick her feet up and enjoy dinner and nice wine. And him.

She looked at the preset menu with the list of recommended wine pairings and grinned as she set it down. "I'm already looking forward to that tiramisu."

"Me too. You deserve a break, and hell, so do I." As alpha, he rarely took off time for himself. But he wanted to make time with Leslie.

41

"I'll definitely drink to that." She reached for the delicate-stemmed wine glass in front of her and lifted it up to him.

He did the same, toasting her.

First the appetizers were brought out and, once they were alone again, he said, "So how are you liking your job? I don't want you to feel pigeonholed, like you have to be stuck in this role if you want to try something else out."

Candlelight flickered between them on the table, playing off the delicate features of her face. Her hair was down today, the curls now a soft wave that he wanted to run his fingers through. "I really like it. I get to set my own schedule and I'm such a numbers nerd. I love math, which I know sounds crazy to a lot of people. You already know that before I lived here, I was an accountant for a few shops downtown. That was before I had to quit." She blinked, looking down at her glass.

Malcolm frowned, not liking that. "Can I ask... ah."

She looked at him again. "It's okay. Ask anything you want."

"How did you and that asshole end up together? Your mom talks about your dad in a way that lets me know they had a true and loving mating before he died."

Sighing, she absently ran her finger along the stem of her glass. "I wish I had a better answer for how I ended up with such a loser. But the short answer is, he fooled me. He fooled everyone. By the time we were mated, it was too late. You know that he threatened my mom—

and that's what took so long for me to leave. Otherwise I would have run immediately. Before that, however, there were no signs. Or if there were, I didn't see them. He didn't get possessive or jealous, and he said he liked that I worked and was so smart.

"All the time, he told me how beautiful I was. Then once we were together, he started to hate the way I would get my hair done or go to the salon to get my nails done. Any type of grooming seemed to annoy the hell out of him. It was like there was this weird shift in his personality, so different from the man I'd mated. He thought I was showing off or trying to attract attention from other males. It was all ridiculous and overbearing. So I went to my alpha, told him I wanted out of my mating."

Malcolm rolled his shoulders. Yeah, he knew she'd gone to her alpha. He'd killed the other alpha—something he'd never told Leslie. It wasn't a secret but it had never come up and it felt odd to tell her. But once she and Luna had run and other packs had gotten wind of the way Leslie's former pack had been treating their she-wolves, all surrounding packs had descended on the male packmates who'd tried to escape the area.

That was shifter justice for you.

"He ran right back to my mate and told him to keep me in line. At first I was so angry at myself for not seeing him for who he was, but I don't feel like such a fool anymore for trusting my alpha."

Malcolm reached across the table. "You're definitely not a fool for trusting your alpha. He should have protected you, should have looked out for you." The male should have taken care of Leslie's former mate for good and made sure his pack was happy.

"I know. I do know that. They were my first pack. My mom roamed with various wolves over the years, so he was my only experience of what an alpha should be like. Seeing how you are with our pack, the difference is so stark. I see what a real pack, a community of wolves, should be like."

"I need to tell you something," he said quietly. Now was definitely the time to tell her, because if she found out some other way that he'd killed her former alpha, then she would wonder why he hadn't told her after this conversation. He didn't want any secrets between them.

She stilled, her fingers going stiff in his grip. But he didn't let her pull away.

"I killed your former alpha. I wasn't there to hunt down those wolves when they attacked Sapphire and Eli, but I went after your alpha when I heard what he'd condoned, what he'd allowed to go on in his pack. He allowed your abuse to continue." And for that, the male had needed to die. He'd been everything a good shifter hated. Malcolm was just glad that Leslie's mom had turned to her oldest friend Sapphire—a she-wolf from another pack that Malcolm was allied with—and asked for help escaping. In turn Sapphire had teamed up with a jaguar named Eli and those two would forever have sanctuary in Malcolm's pack if they ever requested it.

She blinked in surprise, letting out a nervous breath. "I wasn't expecting you to tell me that. And I already know."

Now *he* blinked in surprise. "You do?"

"Yeah. I've known a while. I heard Hudson and Erica talking about it."

"It doesn't bother you?"

She snorted. "Why would it bother me? He deserved what he got. I found out later that other she-wolves had gone to him for help and he'd betrayed them too. I'm glad he's dead. And I don't care what that says about me."

Malcolm started to say more, then their server returned, chattering about the next dish and carrying a new bottle of wine. So he sat back and listened, but his gaze was on Leslie as she watched the human with a bright light in her eyes, clearly interested in what the man was saying.

He loved seeing her so relaxed like this, just enjoying herself. This was the real Leslie, not the scared woman who'd come to his pack a year and a half ago.

And he was going to do everything possible to make sure she never felt afraid again.

* * *

Leslie inhaled the fresh summer air as they approached her cabin hours later. She would never get sick of being outside, surrounded by so much nature under a blanket of brilliant, bright stars. Before, she'd used the woods and running as an escape from an impossible situation. Now, she had a bigger sense of freedom because she'd found safety with her new pack. "I know today was for work, but I had fun." And she hated that it was coming to an end far too quickly.

"I'm glad." Malcolm was walking close to her, closer than was necessary, and she soaked up all of his warmth and dark, wild forest scent.

Something about it reminded her of the Highlands, all wild and free and savagely beautiful. Like him.

"How long has it been since you've been back to Scotland?" He'd lived there long before he came to the States and formed his own pack. His accent was so faint now, having been here for a century, but every now and then she heard hints of it and it warmed her from the inside out.

He glanced at her in surprise as they reached the bottom step of her porch stairs. "Too long. Why?"

"Nothing," she murmured. She didn't want to tell him she was scenting him and dissecting what he smelled like in her head. That sounded weird.

He narrowed his gaze slightly, but thankfully let it drop. On the porch, in front of her door, she felt as nervous as if she were a teenager on a date. Which was just stupid. This had *not* been a date. He was her alpha and he'd asked for her advice with a work thing. He hadn't given her one hint that he was interested in anything more. She needed to get her head out of the clouds and stay firmly grounded in reality. The one where Malcolm was the alpha and she was just a beta packmate. Man, reality sucked.

Malcolm placed his hand against the door as he looked down at her.

Her breath caught in her throat as he watched her carefully, his blue eyes bright even in the darkness. His wolf flashed in his gaze for a second before fading back to human.

She wasn't sure why he was looking at her like that. Like he wanted to claim her.

She was hopeful, yes, but she'd been burned so badly, and the last thing she could stand was embarrassing herself. Because if she made a move on her alpha and he wasn't interested, then he would let her down gently and that would make her feel a thousand times worse. Because then he would just pity her, and she wasn't sure she could recover from that kind of rejection. "Thank you again for today."

"My pleasure." His words were softly spoken, a rumbly growl she felt coursing all the way through her. Good God, she wanted to bottle up his voice, it was so sexy. Then she could listen to it anytime she wanted.

She cleared her throat. "Well... I'm going inside." The air suddenly felt charged, as if something had shifted, but she couldn't get a grip on the change.

His fingers clenched against the door, and she swore he was going to say more but he shoved up, his expression dark as he stepped back. "Look, Leslie, if there's anything you need. Anything," he stressed. "I'm here for you."

"I know." And she did know. He was nothing like her old alpha, and she knew without a doubt that if she went to him with a real problem, he'd do his best to solve it.

"I hope that you do." He turned and headed down the stairs. As he walked off into the darkness, getting swallowed up by the shadows, she shoved out an unsteady breath. All of her muscles were pulled taut as she finally stepped inside.

Before she had any time to dwell on what had just happened, or what had *not* happened, Elijah jumped down from her mom's lap where they'd been sitting on the couch.

"Mama!" he shouted, toddling toward her. He only knew a few words at this point and Mama was his favorite one.

Hers too. She covered the distance between them, scooping him up in her arms. He grabbed the sides of her neck with his chubby little hands in his version of a hug and planted wet kisses on her cheeks.

"Mama, Mama," he said excitedly.

And just like that, the rest of the world faded away. She boxed up all her feelings and confusion about Malcolm and focused on the little boy in her arms.

CHAPTER SIX

Leslie smiled down at Elijah as he babbled incessantly, building his oversized toddler Legos. Every once in a while, he would look up at her, shake his little fist and babble something before looking back down at his creation. She always agreed with whatever he said, which seemed to satisfy the bossy little cutie.

"I never get tired of watching him play," her mom said, walking in from the kitchen, mug of steaming-hot tea in hand as she crouched down on the living room floor next to them.

"I know. He really is the cutest thing in the world." With skin a slightly lighter shade of brown than hers, he had her dark eyes and a little tuft of dark hair covering his head. His arms and legs were chubby, and his cheeks, she could squish all day long. This little guy seriously owned her heart and she wouldn't have it any other way.

They both turned at the sound of a knock on the front door. Before she'd even had a chance to say come in, the door swung open and Chelsea, one of her favorite packmates, marched in as if she owned the place. Her pink-and-purple-dyed hair—which matched her rainbow-colored manicure—was pulled back in a ponytail and she had on her standard fitted cargo pants and a black tank top.

"Did we forget our manners today?" her mom asked mildly.

Chelsea simply stuck her tongue out at Luna, acting like a child herself instead of the one-hundred-plus-year-old shifter she was. "I can't wait. What's going on with you and Malcolm?" Without waiting for a response, she scooped up Elijah, who giggled as she lifted his shirt and started blowing raspberries on his tummy. She didn't even care when he grabbed onto her earring and started tugging.

"We didn't go on a date… And you'd better watch those earrings because he's going to keep going." It was the reason Leslie usually wore studs now instead of her favorite hoops.

Laughing, Chelsea quickly took the dangling gold triangle-shaped earrings out of her ears, then settled Elijah against her side, letting him tug on her ponytail to his heart's content. Shifters definitely had a higher tolerance for pain than humans.

"So wait, you didn't go on a date?"

"We were gone yesterday for a work thing. Why?"

Chelsea threw her head back in mock disappointment. "The whole pack is talking about you two, and I couldn't believe you didn't let me know first."

"Rest assured you're not missing out on any gossip." A little dagger slid through Leslie's chest because she wished yesterday *had* been a date. Instead, things had ended weirdly, and she was still shaken up about it. But he was alpha. If he'd wanted her, he would have made a move. That was simply how it worked in the shifter world. And an alpha or a warrior always, always pursued their future mates. Hard.

Chelsea's eyes narrowed at her. "You were gone most of yesterday, and I know he took you to a vineyard. I've seen the pictures! That was not work. Unless drinking and eating and frolicking around a vineyard is work."

"Did you just say frolic?"

"It's a word, and don't get me sidetracked. I saw the pictures."

"Pictures? Oh, he took some of the vineyard for our files." He'd also decided to take a selfie of the two of them, which had been kind of sweet, if a little out of character for the sexy wolf. He'd been so relaxed yesterday, not the "in charge" alpha who had to make sure the pack remained a well-oiled machine. She wondered how Chelsea had even seen the pictures though.

"It's not nothing. You're just holding out on me."

"No I'm not," she snapped, pushing back that swell of pain she was trying so hard to keep buried. "Trust me, if anything happened between us, I would've let you know. I would have welcomed it! He had the chance to kiss me last night and he didn't take it. He's an alpha. If he wanted me, he would have made it pretty clear."

Ah crap, she hadn't meant to let all that out. But she couldn't stand talking about this and pretending it didn't hurt.

And now her mom was staring at her in surprise, as well as Chelsea. Her friend blinked at her as she extricated another fistful of her hair from Elijah's chubby hands and placed him back on the ground. "Look, I just thought..." Chelsea cleared her throat, all teasing gone from her voice.

And Leslie felt like crap.

Now free, Elijah crawled over to Leslie and curled up in her lap, which eased her heartache a little. He'd already tired himself out this morning and as he settled against her, she kissed the top of his head. "Look, I appreciate gossip just as much as the next wolf, but right now it's too painful to talk about. He doesn't want me. And I get that you think he does, but he doesn't. It's the way it is. And as a friend, I would appreciate you not telling the rest of the pack about my little outburst. I don't want Malcolm feeling like he's got to let me down easy or feeling sorry for poor pathetic Leslie." And she really didn't want to be the subject of gossip.

"No one feels sorry for you," Chelsea said, glancing between her and Luna, who was remaining quiet and watchful.

Feeling suffocated, Leslie gently eased Elijah into her mom's lap. "I'm going for a quick run," she murmured, not caring if she was being rude. She just couldn't be around people anymore. And she couldn't sit here and talk about Malcolm either. It was too much.

She heard Chelsea curse behind her as she hurried out the front door but she needed to be alone, she needed to let her wolf out.

It bothered her deeply that the whole pack was apparently talking about her and Malcolm. It felt so invasive and, more than anything, *embarrassing*. If he was into her, she wouldn't care if they were gossiping about the two of them. But now?

She inwardly groaned. The last thing she ever wanted was for her pack to feel sorry for her. She'd gotten that enough when she'd first moved here, and now she felt like she'd finally found her footing.

She was just Leslie, pack accountant and mom to Elijah. Not poor abused Leslie who'd escaped a monster. She didn't want to become poor sad Leslie who has a crush on the alpha.

Leslie wasn't sure where she was running, but she stripped off her clothes as soon as she ducked behind a large tree and let the shift come over her. Fur replaced skin as her bones realigned in a sharp burst of magic.

She hit the ground running, her paws pounding against the earth as she ran and ran and ran. The property extended for thousands of miles and she knew they bordered another pack, so she didn't head east but west instead.

Cool air rolled over her fur as the sun beat down on her, soothing her battered soul. Her muscles strained at the exertion and she welcomed it. She needed to burn off energy.

To outrun her stupid heartache. She felt like the biggest fool for wanting someone she couldn't have.

She was lucky to be alive, lucky to have a new pack. But she wanted more. Despite everything that had happened, she wanted a full, rich future.

And she wanted it with Malcolm. But he was an alpha and she was a beta wolf. The two of them didn't make sense on paper—didn't make sense at all. Sure, alphas mated with betas, but if he wanted her, she would certainly know it by now.

No. She had to stop thinking about him. If she kept obsessing, then her run would have been for nothing. It was time to get her head on straight.

As she trotted up to a wide-open lake with clear water, she crouched down, then shifted to her human form. No one was around so she stretched out on her back, allowing the sun to completely bathe her in its warmth.

She'd found a good pack for her son. A safe place to live surrounded by truly caring wolves. She needed to remind herself of that.

If Malcolm ever took a mate then she would have to leave, because she wouldn't be able to stand it. She knew that much about herself. But for now, she could live with this. There was a lot she could live with. Even if she didn't want to.

At a rustling sound somewhere behind her in the woods, she jerked up, her body instantly on alert.

Before her former mate's abuse, she hadn't been so jumpy. But ever since then, she'd changed on a deeper level. She'd had to in order to survive. But the dark, masculine scent that drifted on the breeze instantly soothed her even as it made her heart rate speed up.

Instinctively she shifted, letting her wolf take over. Nudity was no big deal to shifters for the most part, but she wasn't going to sit here naked with the man of her fantasies. At least in her wolf form he wouldn't be able to scent the riot of her emotions. Not well, anyway.

A giant brown and gray wolf bounded out of the brush, aiming straight for her.

She knew that if he'd wanted to be quiet, he could have been as stealthy as a jaguar shifter, who were known for their quiet. For such a big wolf, he had an incredible ability to move silently. So he'd announced his presence, not wanting to scare her. Which warmed her from the inside out. He really was thoughtful, everything an alpha should be.

Everything a friend should be.

And that was what he was, a friend.

She trotted up to him and nudged him playfully in the side with her nose. She might be all up in her head right now but her wolf still wanted to play.

He got down low in a play bow, his tail wagging, and if she'd been in human form, she would have laughed at his playful expression.

This was something she'd been missing for so long. Her old pack had gone running together, but there hadn't been much happiness, much playful banter. Because her old pack had been dying; she simply hadn't realized it.

She yipped at him, swatting him gently with her paw before turning and running.

He cut her off quickly because yeah, he was superfast. But then he jumped off her and basically bopped her on the nose with his paw. As if to say *tag, you're it.*

Her heart sang with joy as she chased after him.

It took her longer to catch him but she eventually did. And they played like that for ages, until he motioned that it was time to head back to the compound.

The ache lingered in her chest, but she still felt better. Because she'd been able to spend time with him alone. The run back to the property was beautiful and by the time they made it back to the compound, she was feeling ten times lighter.

Still, when they reached what she thought of as civilization, she scented and then saw a dozen packmates milling around, and they were mostly all in human form. And she wasn't going to get naked in front of her packmates today. She was feeling too raw and vulnerable and up in her own head. So she grabbed her cache of clothing in her mouth and headed back to her cabin.

She assumed Malcolm headed to his because he didn't follow her home.

I can do this, she reminded herself. Even if she only got a little part of him, she would take it.

CHAPTER SEVEN

"So what do you think?" Jared asked Leslie, hands shoved into his pockets as he looked down at her. Tall and good-looking, the dark-haired male was normally a charmer, but right now waves of nervousness rolled off him.

"I read over it and it looks good. You edited everything I suggested from before and it's an impressive proposal. I think it's ready for him to look at." Him, meaning Malcolm.

The very sexy alpha who had been avoiding her for the last two days. Seriously, what was going on with him? After they'd played together in wolf form, he'd been scarce ever since. And a few times she swore she'd seen him out in the woods but once she went looking for him, she couldn't find him. He hadn't been in his office the few times she'd gone to see him either.

Now at a pack party celebrating someone's birthday, she thought for sure he wouldn't be able to avoid her. Turned out she'd been wrong.

He'd been very busy with everyone else but her and it seemed so obvious that he was avoiding her. That part cut deep. It was like he was rejecting her, and she wasn't sure what she'd done to deserve it. But she was putting on a smile and faking her happiness. She'd gotten good at that.

"Okay great, I'm going to talk to him tomorrow about it," Jared said.

"Malcolm will be thrilled to look at it, I'm sure." As if she'd conjured him from her thoughts, Malcolm appeared out of nowhere, but he wasn't looking at her. Instead, he was glaring daggers at Jared. "What will I be thrilled to look at?"

She frowned up at him. "It's a business proposal. He's going to show you tomorrow." She shooed Jared off because of the strange vibes that Malcolm was putting off.

He turned to look at her, his expression unreadable, his blue eyes as beautiful as ever. God, she'd missed him. "You're working with Jared on something?"

"No. He came up with the idea all by himself. He just wanted me to look at the accounting to make sure he wasn't reading the numbers wrong." She poked him once in the abs and had to bite back a sigh at how muscled he was. Tonight he had on a long-sleeve sweater, but he'd pushed the sleeves up so all the Celtic designs and rune tattoos that symbolized his history fighting in the werewolf-vampiric wars and the link to his Scottish clan were visible. She resisted the crazy urge to trace her fingers over the sleek lines. "So go easy on him. He just wants to impress you."

Malcolm reached between them and grabbed her finger. Surprising her, he brought her hand up to his face and basically inhaled her scent.

She stared in shock at the possessive display. Just as quickly, he dropped her hand as if she'd burned him. Then he took a small step backward as if he was going to leave.

Oh no. No way. She grabbed his hand in hers, and he froze. "You and I are going to go talk."

He looked as if he wanted to argue for a millisecond but then nodded and shifted their hands so that he was holding on to her tight. "Lead the way." His words were all gravelly and sexy and she felt them oh so deep.

Ignoring the curious looks from some of their packmates—and the wolf whistles—she dragged him to the edge of the party and then kept going past all the picnic tables, the mini bars that had been set up, and the plethora of balloons and decorative lights. Voices and the music faded in the distance as they walked, and she could admit she liked the feel of his big hand holding hers.

Once she was sure they had enough privacy, she stopped behind one of the office cabins then turned to face him. She put her hands on her hips as she looked up at him.

Under the moonlight, he looked like an avenging angel, a warrior god sent here to mess with all of her senses. "Well?" she demanded.

"Well what?" His tone was carefully neutral.

"What's going on with you? You've been avoiding me for two days. And don't bother to deny it."

"I wasn't going to deny it."

When he admitted that he *had* been avoiding her, it was like a punch to her solar plexus. Oh, wow. That definitely hurt. It was one thing to suspect, but to have him confirm it?

He must have seen the hurt in her expression or just scented it, because he cursed savagely and reached out to cup her cheek. But right before he made contact with her skin, he dropped his hand. "I'm trying to give you space," he rasped out.

"Space from what?"

"Me."

She watched him for a long moment, trying to digest his words. And she wasn't sure she completely understood him. "Why?" She wanted it spelled out for her right now so she didn't make a fool of herself.

He closed his eyes for a long moment then looked up at the blanket of brilliant stars scattered above them. Finally, he met her gaze. "I know you were hurt before. I don't ever want you to be afraid of me."

"Can you be more specific?" she whispered. She really, really did not want to get this wrong. It would hurt too bad if she did.

"I want you more than I've ever wanted anyone. Ever," he said again, as if to make that part clear. "But I'm the alpha and you're fairly new to the pack. I don't ever want you to feel like you owe me or are obligated to me. I've never been in this position before, and I've been going against all my normal instincts. I've been courting you, but—"

Her eyes widened. "What?"

"I thought I'd been obvious about it with all the food gifts over the last six months."

She stared at him as realization set in. She'd been so beat down because of her ex that she'd missed the most obvious sign. Malcolm... *had* been courting her. Very quietly and subtly without pushing or being heavy-handed. "I don't know what to say."

"You don't have to say anything. But now you know where I stand." Surprising the hell out of her, he got to his knees and looked up at her. "I know I'm the alpha, but you are completely in charge right now."

She stared at him with a mixture of fascination and horror. "Get up," she rasped out even as she tugged at him to stand. This was insane, even if it was insanely hot. "You're the alpha, you can't do this."

He grudgingly stood and thankfully he didn't put any distance between them. "I'm just trying to give you space. I'm trying to let you do things in your own time. But I want you to understand that we'll go as slow as you want. I'm not walking away."

It took a long moment for her to digest everything. This was... everything she'd wanted to hear from him. She didn't know what to say or how to feel. Okay, that was a lie. She was nervous as hell because of everything that had happened before, but she knew Malcolm would never hurt her. She also knew the future wasn't guaranteed. Nothing was.

She grabbed the front of his shirt and tugged him down closer to her. She needed this, needed *him*.

"Yes," he said savagely.

"Yes?"

"I've been waiting for you to make the first move. Kiss me," he groaned, and it came out as a plea instead of an order. Somehow it was the sexiest thing she'd ever heard in her entire life.

She was a beta by nature, definitely not as strong or battle-hardened as him. And she had a much more even-tempered personality. Except for right now, because she felt manic and hungry for him. She dug her fingers into his shirt and tugged him the rest of the way down.

Not that he resisted.

The second their lips collided, he took over. It was almost immediate, as if he couldn't help himself, but then he slowed down, taking his time, stroking his tongue against hers in sweet little flicks.

She arched into him, wrapping her arms around his neck even as she practically jumped him, hoisting her legs around his hips. All her muscles were pulled taut, her nerve endings hyperaware of every little place they were touching. It didn't matter that clothing was in the way, he was completely dominating her mouth and she loved it. And she wanted more.

Hunger and lust surged through her as she plastered herself to this male. It had been so damn long since she'd enjoyed the touch of a man. And she somehow knew that she would never enjoy anyone as much as Malcolm.

Suddenly she found her back flat against something and realized he'd moved them to a wall.

She moaned into his mouth as he plundered her own, taking and teasing. This was everything she'd been fantasizing about, everything she wanted. At the feel of his tongue against hers, anticipation hummed, a steady buzz inside her. While she had no clue what the rest of the night held, she knew she wanted more of this. Of him.

His shoulder muscles were bunched tight as she clutched on to him, and his scent had grown wilder and deeper and she wanted to roll around in it. To completely immerse herself in everything Malcolm. He eclipsed everything around them.

But just as quickly as the kiss had started, he pulled back, his breathing harsh and uneven. Closing his eyes, he lay his forehead against hers.

Why had he stopped?

She could scent his lust, the rich, dark scent of it wrapping around her, and it was better than any triple-dipped cashew chocolates.

"So now you know how I feel," he murmured, his voice a deep rumble. "I'm claiming you. But we need to take things slow."

Slow? She was about to protest but he brushed his lips over hers, and she leaned into it.

"Slow," he continued, whether for her benefit or his, she wasn't sure. "You just came off of a bad relationship."

"It was over a long time ago. And it was never real." She'd been a prisoner, not a willing participant.

He looked her in the eyes. "That might be so. But I'm playing for keeps. So I need you to be *very* sure about this."

She nodded, because he was right. He'd just laid a whole lot on her. While she knew that she wanted Malcolm—was insanely attracted to him—she'd also been incredibly wrong in the past.

Her wolf told her everything she needed to know, however. He wasn't going to hurt her. Not Malcolm.

Still, she could tell by his expression that he wasn't going to back down from this. She was only getting this kiss tonight. And that was okay because she knew that soon there would be more. *There better be.* He'd opened up something inside her and there was no way that this could be all there was between them. She wanted all of him.

Sighing, she dropped her legs from around his waist but didn't let go of him. "So what does this mean for us? What are we?"

"Oh, you are mine, sweet wolf."

Heat flared inside her at the possession in his tone. If it had come from anyone else, she would've hated it. But she loved the thought of belonging to Malcolm. "So you and I are… out in the open? No secret courting or anything."

"It wasn't a secret before," he growled. "You just didn't realize what I was doing. What I'm still doing."

She blinked at his rough tone, her nipples tightening at the sound. God, she didn't want to go back to the party, but they better or she was going to start begging for more. "Good... You want to head back to the party?"

"Not really. But it's definitely the wisest choice now," he grumbled, taking her hand in his as they headed back to the laughter and music.

When they stepped back into the fray, they got a few looks at the fact that they were holding hands and, of course, a few juvenile wolves let out whistles, but mostly she got thumbs up from her friends and especially from Chelsea, who mouthed, "I knew it."

The complete lack of surprise from the pack at seeing them together shocked the hell out of her. He really had been courting her, and she just hadn't seen the signs. She'd been so caught up in her own head and the hurt of her past that she hadn't been able to see the future in front of her.

No matter what, she wasn't going to let the past affect her future and happiness.

CHAPTER EIGHT

Hudson strode up Malcolm's porch stairs, two insulated thermoses of coffee in hand. "You and Leslie finally got together?" his brother asked.

It was four in the morning and they had a pack issue to deal with—the only reason they were up at this hour.

Malcolm grunted in appreciation as he took one thermos. "Yep." And that was all he was going to say about it right now. He felt protective and possessive of her in a way he'd never experienced. And after last night, after she knew his intentions and reciprocated, he wasn't going to do anything to screw this up. It had taken every ounce of self-control he possessed not to claim her last night, not to take her right up against the outside of that cabin. After getting a taste of her, finding out exactly how sweet her kisses were, it had been almost impossible to step back. But she deserved better than that. He wanted her to be very, very sure of what she wanted with him. Because he'd been serious—he was playing for keeps.

"Thank God." His brother lifted his own thermos in a toast. "Now on to business. I swear to God, if this is Alex's pack…" Hudson trailed off, his wolf flashing in his eyes briefly, his knuckles going white as they tightened around the thermos.

"I know." They'd both received a call barely five minutes ago from one of the sentries out patrolling. There had been a sighting of a wolf on the property. A wolf shifter who wasn't pack. And there was no way that wolf shifter had gotten lost. It was almost impossible to stumble on their territory unless you came from the direction of the mountains. And again, that was pretty close to impossible, considering their territory spanned for thousands of miles.

So now they were heading out to meet up with the sentries in charge of security for this shift.

"Check it out," Hudson said, motioning to the souped-up ATV he'd arrived in.

"When'd you get this done?" The custom paint job looked damn good. The camouflage would blend perfectly out in the woods.

"I hired that human in town to do it. He nailed it too." Hudson took a sip of his coffee, but watched Malcolm over the rim of the thermos, amusement in his gaze.

He knew exactly what human his brother was talking about—the one who'd taken Leslie out on a date. But he wasn't going to be baited this morning, so he shrugged.

Hudson just snickered as he got in the driver's seat. It was already idling, with a pack of supplies in the back. Normally they would go in wolf form but it seemed his brother had decided to drive this morning. Which was fine with him.

He needed coffee anyway.

As if he read his mind, Hudson said, "I packed some food and coffee for the crew."

"Good." They all rotated out with who worked nights and days, but it still sucked to work the long shift.

It didn't take long to get to the meeting point a couple miles away.

"So what do we have?" Malcolm jumped out of the ATV before Hudson had fully stopped, and approached Amber and Heath.

Amber, the older of the two by about fifty years, was in charge of this shift. She stepped forward, her expression grim. "He's an old wolf for sure. He's gray and white and big—as big as you," she said to Malcolm. "I could feel the power rolling off him. We both tried approaching him on two separate occasions, and he ran off. But he didn't run because he was scared, of that I'm certain. I think he's scouting our territory. Maybe for another alpha or…" She shrugged. "Who knows?"

Malcolm nodded as he digested this. "Did he smell familiar?"

"No."

"If you see him again, keep an eye on him, but don't outright attack unless you have no choice." Technically he was within his rights to kill any intruder on pack territory. Those were shifter rules. But he would prefer to talk to the wolf first. Especially since the wolf hadn't been aggressive so far. There could be a reason he was on Kendrick property, but Malcolm couldn't think of a good one. "I'm going to let Alex know too."

Walking away, he pulled out his cell phone, not caring how early it was. Alex was an alpha, he was used to getting early-morning calls and alerts. And as his neighboring alpha, alerting him to any issues was part of the alliance they had in place so Malcolm owed him this call immediately.

"What's up?" Alex answered on the second ring.

"We scented a strange wolf shifter on our property. My sentries have tried to approach him a couple times, to no avail." Then he ran down the physical description of the wolf.

"It's not one of mine."

"I know. I didn't think it was." They'd had an issue with Alex's pack last year but it was more of an internal thing, where a bunch of teenagers had been acting out and thinking they were tougher than they were. "I just wanted to give you a heads up."

"Appreciate it. And if I see him, I'll let you know."

"Thanks. Have you had any issues in general with anything?" Malcolm asked.

"No. The pack is settled back to normal. My cousin left with his troublemaking friends. Last I heard they were in the Caribbean, getting into trouble." There was a note of annoyance and disgust in Alex's tone. "I should have kicked them out a long time ago."

"Not your problem anymore."

"Amen to that. So… I hear you're getting mated?" Alex asked.

Damn, word traveled fast. It made sense though because many of the she-wolves from each of their packs were friends. And most of the she-wolves from Alex's pack now frequented Erica's relatively new salon. Opening the salon was one of the best things that had ever happened for the unity of their two packs.

He might like and respect Alex, but he wasn't talking about Leslie with him. "If that's all then, I'll talk to you later."

Alex snorted. "All right then."

Once they disconnected, he glanced around the quiet woods. It might not be his shift, but he didn't give a shit. This was his pack and his territory.

Moving quickly, he stripped and changed. He was going to go on a hunting expedition. He didn't like the thought of a strange wolf in his territory ever, and especially not now.

Not when he had his future mate to protect.

CHAPTER NINE

"So what happened this morning?" Leslie asked as she set a plate of mashed fruit in front of Elijah, who was sitting in his highchair and babbling at Malcolm.

Malcolm had come over for lunch today but she'd already heard through the grapevine that he and Hudson had gone out on patrol early because of some kind of disturbance. He must be tired, but she couldn't tell it to look at him. In a short-sleeved T-shirt, cargo-type pants and heavy boots, he just looked good enough to eat. Like always.

"Our sentries spotted a strange wolf in the territory. They saw him a couple times and he avoided approaching any of them. Could be any number of things. Someone passing through, someone sniffing out our territory." He shrugged. "I don't want to talk about that though. What are *you* doing tonight?" His blue eyes flashed to pure wolf for a moment before flashing back.

"I don't have any plans. But if a certain sexy wolf asks me out, I'm in." Oh, she was so in. And she hoped those plans included them getting naked. She wasn't sure if she was ready for full-on sex, but that didn't mean they couldn't have fun and explore each other.

He grinned at her. "I'll pick you up here at six, if that works?"

She nodded. "As long as my mom can watch Elijah—and I can't see her saying no."

Elijah, who had clearly decided he didn't like *not* being the center of attention, squealed and threw a piece of banana over the edge of his highchair.

Malcolm picked it up and set it on the table to be thrown away.

Elijah shoved a piece of banana in his mouth, then took another piece and threw it off the edge of the highchair again, intently watching Malcolm as he did it. Not challenging, but curious.

When Malcolm bent down to pick it up again, he laughed, spitting banana out and shaking his fists in the air as if this was the funniest thing in the world.

"If you keep doing it, he's going to keep throwing food on the floor." She sat down next to him, so that she could watch both Malcolm and Elijah.

Malcolm grinned. "I know. I just don't care."

Elijah took a little handful of banana and held it over the highchair, then stopped and put it back on the tray. But then a second later tossed it over and looked away as if he hadn't done it. Then he started giggling maniacally as Malcolm bent down to pick it up.

"He's the cutest baby who was ever born," she said, knowing full well she was biased.

"I know. I love having pups around again."

She did too, and she was glad that Elijah was going to grow up with other pups in a safe, happy pack. There were at least ten in the pack right now, and a few other females were currently pregnant. Something was definitely in the water and she was grateful for it. She also loved the interaction between Malcolm and her son. Seeing how easy he was with him, how patient he was, it warmed up everything inside her.

There was very clearly no comparison between her abusive ex and Malcolm—because Malcolm would win every time—but it was difficult not to compare the differences between the two.

She could just imagine how angry her ex would have gotten at the mess on the floor. He wouldn't have sat here laughing and playing games. No, he would've taken his anger out on her, yelling at her to clean it up. Not that she would have stayed around that long, but it was easy to envision it playing out.

Being here with Malcolm right now felt so right. Still, she couldn't help her nerves, couldn't help but worry in general. She'd gotten burned so badly before and it had taken a toll on her self-esteem, on everything. Even the way she reacted to situations.

Though becoming a mother had helped her bounce back quicker than anything else ever could have. It was difficult to get completely swallowed up in your own head when you had a helpless little person to take care of.

"What are you thinking about right now?" Malcolm's deep voice pulled her out of her thoughts as she turned to look at him.

"Just thinking about how I like watching you two together."

In response, he leaned over, brushing his lips against hers.

She felt his kiss spread through her, completely warming her cheeks. Malcolm eclipsed everyone and every other kiss she'd ever had, even with the soft way his lips grazed hers now.

Elijah started squealing at that moment and when she turned to look at him, he was grinning at her, his chubby cheeks so kissable. So she leaned over and kissed him as well.

"I didn't forget about you, little man." She kissed his other cheek, which made him giggle and take her cheeks in his little hands. His banana-covered hands.

"Love Mama."

"I love you too." She kissed him on the nose for good measure.

"He's lucky to have you," Malcolm said as she sat back and started wiping off her face.

"I'm lucky to have *him*." She cleared her throat. "Can I ask you something?"

"Of course."

"I don't even know exactly how to say this… But if we do move forward in our relationship," she couldn't say the words "get mated" just yet, "then Elijah would be yours as well." It was such a different situation with Malcolm as opposed to any other wolf, because he was alpha of the pack. He already took care of everyone to an extent, but it would be different with Elijah.

He nodded slowly. "I understand that you two are a package deal. I want to be in his life too. I want to be in *both* your lives."

"I know. I'm just thinking of the far-flung future and all of these what-ifs come into my head."

He nodded in understanding. "Ah, like what if we have pups? Is that what you're thinking?"

She nodded. It was too weird for her to voice that particular thing aloud, but yes, that was exactly what she'd been thinking about. Malcolm had made it clear that he wanted her, but fear still lived inside her no matter how much she tried to shove it back down.

"If we do, I will love all of them the same. He doesn't have to be my blood to love him as my own."

She knew that on every level, but she suddenly realized she'd needed to hear the words. And that simple statement from him eased the tension inside her. "Okay then."

"Okay?"

"I believe you." And she did. Malcolm was a man of his word, and she could see the love in his eyes every time he played with Elijah.

He leaned over, kissing her again. "Tonight needs to get here faster," he growled against her mouth.

She laughed lightly even as she fought the shivers of delight humming through her. The anticipation building in her was already at volcanic levels. "Too bad I have to work and you've got a bunch of meetings today."

"How do you know that?"

"Well, the fact that there are rarely any secrets here is part of the reason, but a couple of our packmates came to me with different business proposals for you. You already know about Jared, but there are a couple others, and I know they're meeting with you today."

He gave her a thoughtful look and simply nodded before brushing his lips over hers again.

But once again, he pulled back before she could even think about deepening it. And oh, how she wanted to.

She could be patient, however. She hoped.

CHAPTER TEN

"Thank you for coming over tonight," Leslie said to her mom, who already had Elijah cuddled up in her arms.

"You don't need to thank me for taking care of my grandson. Have fun tonight. You deserve this." She smiled down at Elijah, who was playing with her braids.

"You don't think it's too soon?"

Her mom lifted a shoulder. "It's never too soon to start living again. You know my philosophy on life. Don't waste time worrying about what other people think. You get one life, make it count."

"True." Leaning forward, she kissed her mom on the cheek before heading out. She did indeed know her mom's philosophy.

Her mom and her aunt Sapphire—who wasn't technically related to her but might as well be—had grown up with their hippie parents, traversing the world. The only reason her mom had ever settled down at all had been because of Leslie's dad. Apparently they'd been opposites in many ways, including him being a bit more serious and a numbers nerd just like Leslie. So at least she knew where she'd gotten her love of math.

She loved running wild in her wolf form but she'd never had that urge to go roaming around the world like some wolves did. And now that she had a pup, she didn't think she would ever get that urge.

Though she definitely had the urge to get naked with Malcolm. So very naked.

"Did you forget about our date?" Malcolm slid out of the shadows like the sneaky wolf he was as she reached the bottom step.

Yeah right. It was all she'd been thinking about—obsessing about in the best way possible. She wasn't sure what was going to happen tonight, but she'd chosen her lingerie carefully, that was for sure. "No. I knew you'd be early, so I figured I'd meet you out here." He laughed lightly, and that was when she spotted the picnic basket in his hand. "We're going on a picnic?" That was absolutely adorable.

"It's still light enough out." He pointed to the ATV she knew was Hudson's baby. "We can shift, or take that."

"Let's go in the ATV. I've never been in it before."

He lifted an eyebrow at her in surprise.

She shrugged. "I've never had a reason to ride in it." At the word "ride," she suddenly thought of riding him and then nearly tripped in surprise. It was as if his kisses, his admission of what he wanted with her, had awakened something inside her. Now getting naked with him was all she could think about.

He shot her a sideways glance, as if he scented her lust, but that was okay because she scented his too. He definitely wasn't trying to hide it. "Have you ever been on the four-wheelers before?" he asked as they headed toward the two-seater ATV that looked more like a giant golf cart to her than anything.

"No." Though she'd seen the sentries taking them out and acting like crazy teenagers on them instead of the trained warriors they were.

"Then you and I are definitely going to remedy that. We'll take them out this weekend if you want."

"Sounds good to me. I finished up a bunch of your accounting reports early for you, so we'll have time." He wouldn't have seen it yet, but she'd sent him an email. "Now you don't have to worry about them." She'd finished her work early today and had decided to sneak into his files and update a bunch of things. He was woefully slow about his accounting and she'd wanted to do something nice for him. He'd been courting her for six months and she hadn't even noticed. Well, she'd noticed all the food gifts, but she hadn't connected the dots and realized what he'd been doing.

He took her mouth in a fast, breathtaking kiss. "You are the best," he murmured against her lips.

She arched into him, wanting to tell him to forget the damn picnic and head back to his place. His arms settled around her tightly as he tugged her close, the feel of his erection unmistakable. Yep, forget the picnic.

But then a loud whistle pierced the air, disturbing the moment.

Breathless, she pulled back to see both Ursula and Chelsea striding across the middle of the compound, a.k.a. the grassy area and picnic tables in between a bunch of their cabins.

She smiled at them. They smiled right back but kept going, deep in conversation about something.

"It's a little weird, adjusting," she said as they got into the ATV, her lips tingling from the feel of his mouth on hers.

"What is?"

"Me, you, *us*. I don't know, this is weird. A new stage of our lives and my brain is slowly catching up to this new reality." Her brain and body both. It was like she'd been living in this cave or in a cocoon and now? Now, she wanted to bust out of it. She just needed to shake off the stupid fears still lingering in the back of her mind. Malcolm wasn't her ex. He was light-years better, and she knew he would never hurt her in the way her ex had. He wasn't capable of it.

He glanced at her, his blue eyes flashing with heat. "Good weird, I hope."

"Definitely good weird." And that was enough of that. She had to get out of her head. "So what's in the basket?" She turned around and started to open it but he put his hand on top of hers.

"No way. You have to wait. It's a surprise." His grin was mischievous, far more feline than the wolf he was.

She groaned. "You're one of those wolves who wraps Christmas presents like a month early, right? And then proceeds to torture people?"

He snorted. "Definitely. Let me guess, you're like Hudson, who's impatient and doesn't like surprises."

She flashed him a grin. "Guilty. I used to think it was at odds with my numbers-focused brain, but I simply like everything neat and tidy and in order. I like to know what's coming at me. Which I know is impossible because we can't predict the future."

"You can look if you want," he said, smiling as they rumbled over the dirt path.

"Nah. I want to be surprised this time. But fair warning, if you do wrap Christmas presents a month early, there's a good chance I will sneak and open them, and then rewrap them."

He gave her a sideways glance as he expertly maneuvered the steering wheel. "Then I'll have to make sure I hide them well."

It was nice to be talking about their future as if it was a real thing. And she knew it could be. She wanted it; she was just nervous about, well, everything lately. But not too nervous to take a chance on them.

The sun was about an hour from setting, not that it mattered for them since they had night vision and the ATV had headlights. She knew that they wouldn't be going far, anyway. He knew how she felt about not being too far from Elijah at any given point. He was way too young for her to be comfortable a long distance from him. Taking that trip to the winery had stretched her limits for a while.

Ten minutes later, they'd settled on a perfect spot close to the same lake they'd played near the other day, and Malcolm refused to let her help set up anything. It was kind of nice sitting back and letting him do everything, even if it felt weird. She was going to have to come to terms with the fact that yes, he was the alpha, but he was also simply a male wolf courting her, so things were on a different level. Though nothing about their relationship felt simple, it just felt wonderful and exciting.

"I'm impressed." She stretched out her legs on the oversized blanket as he continued pulling different food out of the basket.

There was lots of fruits, cheese—so many different cheeses!—and of course chocolates. "It looks like you picked all my favorites." Because of course he did. He was always thinking of her, and that realization changed everything. Her heart melted a little bit more right then and there as a cool breeze rolled up over the lake, rustling her hair and the edges of the blanket.

He simply grinned at her and pulled out a bottle of wine with the label of the winery the pack was purchasing. She remembered it because it had been her favorite there as well. Apparently he was very good at listening and watching, and she melted a little more. She wasn't used to this at all and it was... a little terrifying on one level. She was almost afraid to get used to it in case something went wrong later.

"Here," he said after he'd poured them both glasses. "To us."

Yes, she definitely liked the sound of that. As they gently touched their glasses together, she heard his phone buzzing but he ignored it. For a moment, she tensed, worried that maybe he should get it. But it was clear that his focus was on her. All right then, if he was going to ignore it, she was too. The flavor of the wine was fruity and bold. And right now, she was feeling bolder than normal.

"I have a confession to make," he murmured.

She froze for a moment, but the sensual look in his eyes told her this was the good kind of confession. Or at least not a bad one. "Is it that you're going commando?" she teased, hoping that he was.

His expression went even more heated as he growled low in his throat. Reaching for her hand, he gently stroked his thumb over her palm. "I am, but that's not what I meant. I'd already put in an offer for the winery when I asked you to come with me. I just wanted to spend time with you."

Yep, she was melting even more. "I think I can live with that," she murmured, laughing lightly at his "confession". That day had been so much fun and she'd treasured the time with him. "I have a confession too... I loosened the washer under my sink last time because I wanted to see you." She bit her bottom lip, fighting a laugh. "I didn't the other times, and I know it was wrong, but I'm not sorry. I just really wanted to see you."

He blinked once before his mouth curved up wickedly. "I can definitely live with that."

She set the drink down and, feeling unnaturally bold, crawled across the blanket until she was practically on top of him. She paused, unsure exactly what she wanted. Okay, she knew what she wanted, but she was in uncharted territory. It was out of character for her to take the lead, but she really wanted to get this right.

His hands were planted on the blanket at his sides, the muscles in his forearms pulled tight as he grasped onto the blanket—as if he was fighting not to grab her. He sat frozen, watching her with unbridled hunger. "You can do whatever you want," he rasped out as if he'd actually read her mind.

She was feeling so out of her depth with him and while she knew he wanted her, this boldness was new for her. But Malcolm's words eased the tension coiled in her belly. So she straddled him, settling perfectly on top of him and loving the way they fit together. His leg muscles bunched tight under her, his raw power humming through the air as if it was an actual tangible thing.

He wrapped his arms around her loosely, his smile soft and sensual while his scent was wicked. "I like you on top of me."

Yeah, she did too, and more than food or wine, she wanted to taste *him*. So she did. As she leaned forward, he met her halfway, and she got exactly what she wanted. A full-on make-out session with Malcolm.

He teased his tongue against hers before gently nipping at her bottom lip. She felt years younger and lighter as they learned each other, just sinking into all the wonderfulness that was him. She had responsibilities, but at the moment it was nice to simply be a woman with the man she wanted, to simply enjoy and get lost in his kisses, his taste and his rich, sensual scent, which was even stronger now. It wrapped around her, embracing her and making her light-headed.

She shifted slightly, moving over his hard length in a long stroke. It didn't matter that they had clothes on, the feel of his thick erection between them was impossible to miss—and she loved his reaction to her. He groaned as she moved against him, rolling his hips up to meet her strokes. Oh God, she could just imagine how thick he would be inside her, and she grew even wetter at the images playing in her mind. Being on top of him like this made her feel heady and powerful in a way she never had.

When his phone buzzed again—and then again—she groaned and pulled back from his kisses, but didn't get off him because she couldn't bear to be separated from him. She was pretty sure if she tried, he wouldn't let her anyway because his grip around her tightened and he growled low in his throat.

"I can hear your phone, and I know you can too."

His jaw clenched tight, his eyes flashing wolf. "I told Hudson that I wasn't to be disturbed. By anyone. He knows we're out right now."

"So that means if he's trying to get ahold of you, it's important. And if you don't answer, he'll probably hunt you down." Considering that she was ninety-nine percent sure that they'd been about to lose all their clothing, she really didn't want to get caught in a naked situation by his brother.

He sighed in resignation but the tension in his body heightened even more. "I've never hated being alpha more than I do right now."

"If you're worried about me it's okay. I get what a huge responsibility you have. I'm not angry or anything." Disappointed, yeah, but she wouldn't make him feel bad about this. She loved how much he cared for their pack. And she knew that this wasn't over. Just postponed.

"I just want to enjoy you right now," he growled, tightening his grip around her again.

Oh, she did too. She wanted him stretched out on his back for her to kiss and touch everywhere. "See what he wants at least. You'll feel better once you check."

He tightened his grip around her with one arm, keeping her in place as he pulled out his cell phone.

Her shifter hearing was excellent so she heard everything clearly. And after a minute, she knew that they were going to have to cut their date short because that strange wolf had been roaming around the property and had killed a few regular wolves—non-shifters. He hadn't taken the meat, either, just left them for dead. That was a violent, savage type of thing that only ferals did. And if this wolf had gone feral, Malcolm would definitely have to get involved. It was a matter of responsibility.

"Tighten security around the compound," he ordered Hudson. "Make sure everything is secure. I'll meet you at the south-side pond. But I need to take Leslie home first."

Once he got off the phone, she said, "I can drive the ATV back. You can just run in wolf form, which I'm sure you'd rather do anyway." They were far too close to the pack's cabins for the feral wolf to be anywhere near them, so she wouldn't have to worry about running across the stranger.

Malcolm shook his head as he eased her off of him and let out a frustrated groan. "Nope. I'm making sure you get back home safely."

"Malcolm "

"This isn't up for discussion."

She stiffened at his imperious tone as she started packing up the food.

He shoved out a sigh. "Right now I'm in alpha mode, and yes, I need to make sure you get home safe because you mean everything to me. You're also pack to me. I would do this with any other packmate."

She narrowed her gaze. "Even Hudson?"

He snorted. "You know what I mean."

"Yeah, I do. I'll try and save you some chocolate, but no promises on the cheese."

He barked out a laugh before kissing her again.

"You better hurry back to me," she murmured against his mouth. Because they weren't close to done.

His eyes were pure wolf then. "Believe it."

CHAPTER ELEVEN

Malcolm strode across the compound, heading toward Leslie's cabin before he even realized where he was going. His instinct simply said "go in that direction" and he wasn't planning to ignore it. He paused, however, nodding at one of his sentries who was heading home, and pulled out his cell phone.

It was after midnight, so he needed to text her first.

He didn't care that he was exhausted after tracking down all the dead animals. His shifter and human sides were enraged that someone would slaughter innocent wolves like that. And it had definitely been that shifter. The scent on the dead animals had been distinct, the same one he and his brother had scented before on their territory.

Right now, everyone was on the lookout and he'd beefed up security around the compound. It was clearly a threat, but some of the animals had been found on Alex's land as well, so they weren't certain if the threat was pack specific.

The stranger had to be feral. When their brains started to decompose, they started killing wildlife first.

His fingers flew across the screen as he texted Leslie. He was surprised he could even text, he was so amped up to see her. *Are you up? If so, do you want company?* If she was asleep and didn't answer... he didn't know what he'd do.

She texted back almost immediately. *Yes and yes.* Then she added a bunch of emojis, which made him smile.

He didn't love all of technology but he could admit that phones were pretty great. He quickly jogged up her porch stairs and before he'd knocked, the door swung open.

In a little pajama set of skimpy shorts and a low-cut, form-fitting tank top that made his eyes go wide, she stepped back.

"Elijah asleep?" he murmured, stepping inside. He assumed so because it was so late, but babies didn't always sleep when they were supposed to. Maybe it made him selfish, but he hoped the little guy was asleep.

"That sweet baby is out for the rest of the night. He ate more than any child should and then basically passed out." She shook her head, her love for Elijah clear.

While Malcolm loved the kid, he was glad he'd get alone time with her. His entire being craved her so he simply gathered her into his arms and held her tight, inhaling deeply as he buried his face against her hair. He loved being able to come to her now, to lean on her, not go back to his cabin. Alone.

She returned his embrace. "Rough night?"

"It wasn't great." He quickly replayed everything to her as she led him into the kitchen and started pulling out the foodstuff he'd packed for their picnic earlier. He didn't want to talk about it at the moment—not when he'd rather get her flat on her back—but he also didn't want to just jump her the second he walked through the door. She deserved better than that. "It's okay, I'm not hungry," he said before she could pull anything else out.

"You sure?" she asked, her fingers wrapped around one of the plastic containers in the fridge.

"I'm hungry for something else." So damn hungry.

Her eyes flared at that, going pure wolf before flashing back to dark brown. She shoved the food back in the fridge and turned to face him, the scent of her lust punching through the air. "We have to be quiet."

And that was all the affirmation he needed. He was out of his chair and had lifted her up in his arms before she could blink. His wolf growled in approval. This was exactly where she belonged.

"I'm not sure what I'm ready for tonight," she whispered. There was a hint of vulnerability in her expression that clawed at him. He could scent her lust, but that didn't mean she was ready to say yes to everything.

"We'll do whatever you want. However much or little. I don't care. I just want to learn what you like, what makes you feel good." He wanted everything from her, but he would wait until she was ready. He needed her to trust him completely with all things, including her body. Especially her body.

All tension fled her shoulders as she wound her arms tighter around his neck.

Moving quickly, he carried her to her bedroom. He knew where it was because he'd helped oversee the construction of all the cabins so many years ago, but her scent alone would have led him to it. Those light undertones of lavender got stronger the closer they got to her room.

He wasn't surprised to find one side of the bed with the covers rumpled, and a book and what smelled like chamomile tea on the nightstand. "Were you up waiting for me?"

She nodded as he set her down by the bed. "Of course. I know you can take care of yourself, but I couldn't sleep until I knew you were okay."

It mattered to him that she'd cared. Not that he'd expected any less, but it still mattered nonetheless that she'd actually been waiting for him, thinking of him.

Because he was so far gone for her, and even tonight when he'd been out doing his job, she hadn't been far from his mind the entire time he'd been out hunting that feral wolf.

"Flat on your back," she ordered him, her voice trembling as she watched him carefully.

Hell yeah. She might be nervous, but she was still into this. "Should I stay clothed?" he asked.

It definitely surprised her, given her wild scent and the way her eyes flared. And to his surprise, she whispered, "Naked."

Oh hell. Slowly, he stripped his shirt off, tossing it who cared where. Her eyes tracked his every move so he kept his gaze pinned on her as he shucked his jeans just as quickly.

Her eyes widened slightly as they landed on his thick erection, and yeah, he liked that she enjoyed what she saw. Because he could scent her lust as it infused the room, mixing with his own to the point that it overwhelmed everything else.

Though it was his instinct to take over, he held back. He was going to do this right. Doing as she'd ordered, he stretched out on her soft, pale purple sheets. Everything about this room was feminine except him. He liked being around her things, surrounded by everything that was soft and sweet and pure Leslie.

It felt weird to give up control like this, but he liked the way she was watching him as if she could devour every inch of him. And he loved the way she was crawling up his body right now even if she was still wearing that skimpy little tank top and shorts. He wanted her completely naked too, but he understood that was going to take time and trust.

She settled over him, her skimpy shorts the only thing separating them as she grinded down on his cock.

Oh, hell. His erection pulsed with need. He grasped her hips as he pushed up, desperate to kiss her, needing as much skin to skin as he could get. Her kisses were making him crazy, but for once, he let a woman take the lead.

He wouldn't do this forever, but damn, he liked this side of Leslie. And he wanted her so comfortable with him that when he *did* take control, there would never,

ever be a hint of fear or hesitation in her beautiful eyes. Because that would kill him. He wanted to have her back, to be the one male she always turned to no matter what. The one male she trusted with her body and her heart.

She broke the kiss and shimmied down his body until she knelt between his legs. Her fingernails slightly dug into his thighs as she looked up at him, all heat and hunger in her gaze.

He forced himself to remain still as she looked down at his cock—which seemed to have a mind of its own. He rolled his hips slightly, his erection thick and heavy between his legs. "Like what you see?" he growled, unable to keep the desperation out of his voice. He wanted her mouth and hands on him. Hell, he wanted more than that.

She gave him a cheeky grin as she slowly wrapped her fingers around his hard length. "Oh yeah. I like this a lot."

Fuck yeah. He jerked under her delicate hold—which quickly grew firmer, bolder. As she began stroking him, he lost the ability to think straight. Her strokes were hard and sure, making him absolutely crazy. Gone was the nervous female from before with the trembling voice. She was confident as she brought him pleasure, and when she dipped her head down and sucked him in, he nearly lost his mind at the sensation.

This was Leslie, the female he'd been fantasizing about for far too long. The feel of her hot, wet mouth on him was enough to make his brain short-circuit. This was everything he'd fantasized about and better. Leslie was everything, and he could hardly believe this was happening after so long.

He clenched his jaw as he slid his fingers through her hair. He didn't hold too hard, didn't want her to think he was trying to take over or force her, but he needed to touch her even more as she pleasured him. She set a pace that was absolute perfection, driving him right to the brink of release. He held off as long as he could, but after fantasizing about her for over a year...

"Leslie." Her name was a prayer and a moan on his lips. "I'm gonna come," he growled. He wanted to give her the option to do what she wanted to.

In response, she simply sucked faster and that was what sent him over the edge. He finally let go of all of his control, coming hard. Because right now she was completely in control of him and he loved every second of it. Somehow he managed to bite back his groans, to stay quiet, but just barely.

When he was completely sated, his body shaking, she lifted her head, a grin on her face. "You're hot when you come," she murmured, crawling up his body and straddling his hips as she draped herself over him. God, he loved the feel of her body on his, and he hated that there was any sort of clothing between them. He needed to be skin to skin with her.

Unable to find his voice just yet, he reached up and threaded his fingers through the back of her hair, cupping her head as he leaned up to kiss her senseless. He wanted more of her. "Let me taste you, let me go down on you," he finally got out. He wanted to be inside her, wanted to thrust deep and imprint himself on her, but it was pretty clear she wasn't ready for that. That was completely fine. But he needed to bring her pleasure. Needed to give her as much as she'd given him. More even.

She paused, and he could scent how much she wanted it. When she finally nodded, the twisted knot of tension inside him eased. He loved that she trusted him enough with her body.

It took him no time at all to get her undressed, his hands actually shaking as he stripped off what little clothing she had. And when he pulled the shorts off, he realized she'd had nothing else underneath, which was insanely hot. He wondered if she always went bare or if tonight was special.

"You humble me," he murmured, stretching out on top of her, but careful not to put all his weight on her.

For a brief moment, he saw her nerves kick in, but then she settled against him and skated her fingers down his chest and over his abs. His muscles bunched under her soft touch and when she started to go lower, he pulled his hips back. "No way, it's my turn."

"Okay, tease." She kept her hands on him, her fingers roaming everywhere, as if she wanted to touch all of him.

He felt the same, that driving need to kiss and mark every part of her overwhelming. He laughed lightly at her words, loving how much he could be himself with her. Hell, he just loved her.

It was way too soon to tell her, but he knew how he felt. And it wasn't changing. She was it for him. His wolf had chosen even before he had, and his wolf was very smart.

Needing to take his time with her, to give her the foreplay she deserved, he kissed her slowly and deeply before he started feathering kisses along her neck. After each kiss, he gently raked his canines against her soft skin, driving her crazy if the way she squirmed and shifted against the sheets was any indication.

Good. He wanted her all worked up by the time he made his way between her legs.

And he was savoring every second of this. Taking his time with her breasts, he sucked on each brown nipple until she finally begged him to stop his torture.

He only did because he was far more interested in tasting between her legs. He felt as if they'd been building up to this for almost a year. Longer for him, really.

Her legs trembled slightly, but she spread her thighs as he leaned down between them. He placed his hands on her inner thighs, keeping them open as she instinctively tried to close her legs. Feeling possessed, he inhaled deeply, her rich, sweet scent something he was already addicted to.

Go slow, he ordered himself.

At the first taste of her on his tongue—and her own muffled cry of pleasure—he groaned in bliss. Then he forced himself to tone it down because he belatedly remembered they needed to be quiet. He didn't want any interruptions because she was going to come at least twice tonight.

He teased his tongue along her slick folds, enjoying the way she rolled her hips against his face and her soft, breathy little sounds of pleasure. She might have been through a lot, but she was fully secure in her body right now, enjoying everything he was doing to her. And her confidence was sexy.

"Just like that," she whispered.

Her body was responsive but he liked the vocal encouragement. Hell, he could listen to her talk all day, but in that passion-roughened voice, it made him hard all over. As he teased along her folds, over and over, he oh-so slowly slid a finger inside her tight sheath.

She grabbed his head and for a moment he thought she was pushing him away, so he stilled.

"No, don't stop." A throaty, ordered growl from a she-wolf in charge.

He smiled against her slick folds. Oh, he wasn't stopping. He slid another finger inside her, enjoying how tight she was and imagining how perfect she would feel when he finally pushed his cock inside her.

"Faster," she groaned. "More, something. You're killing me."

He growled against her folds and then focused on her clit. He would tease her later. Now, he needed her to come, needed to let her take the edge off. He started moving his fingers in and out of her, her inner walls tightening, milking him with each stroke.

Simultaneously he continued teasing her clit, that little bundle of nerves all swollen and beautiful.

His cock was already hard again, a heavy thickness between his legs, but he didn't care. Right now was all about her.

Her hips were going wild as she writhed against his face until she finally fell into orgasm, her climax hitting sharp and fast.

But he was ready for it.

He kept the pressure up on her clit, savoring the sounds of her groans until finally she grabbed his head, her fingers digging in. "Enough," she rasped out.

He eased off, kissing her lower abdomen gently before he crawled up her lean body. When their mouths were only inches apart, he looked down at the woman who'd stolen his heart and was thankful to any and all deities that he'd finally found his mate.

"I'm not done with you," he growled out.

"Good." She reached between their bodies and wrapped her fingers around his cock. Her eyes were heavy-lidded. "Because I'm not done with you either."

No doubt about it, he had definitely died and gone to heaven.

CHAPTER TWELVE

Leslie walked into her kitchen to the delicious smells of sausage, eggs and a rich coffee blend—and her heart stopped at the sight of Elijah and Malcolm talking to each other. Well, Malcolm was talking, and Elijah was doing a lot of nodding and playing with his food.

And Malcolm looked damn fine at the stovetop with his shirt off and his back muscles and various Celtic tattoos proudly on display. His family crest was on his back as well as some other symbols that recognized packmates lost during the last war—he'd given her an education last night on all his tattoos and she'd kissed every one of them. Twice.

"Good morning," she murmured. It was weird to wake up and have Elijah already taken care of. She actually couldn't believe she'd slept in without hearing or even smelling anything until now. It was a little after eight o'clock and she was normally up at six—because that was when Elijah woke up like clockwork.

But Malcolm had given her four orgasms last night so she'd been knocked out in the best way possible.

"Morning, sleepyhead." Malcolm glanced over his shoulder from the stove and gave her a heated look she felt all the way to her core.

Oh yeah, she could definitely get used to this every morning—and she wanted to. She smiled back at him, feeling suddenly shy as she tightened her robe around her. Not trusting anything that came out of her mouth yet, she headed for the coffeepot and poured herself a drink. After adding creamer, she sighed in appreciation of that first sip. "Has he been good for you?" she asked, gently kissing the top of Elijah's head. And dodging a flying piece of cheese.

"He's been great—and loud. I actually can't believe you didn't wake up before now. He's very lively in the morning."

She snorted and sat down at the kitchen table. "He's very lively all day. If he's awake, it's like he has a tiny engine inside him that rarely quits."

Now Malcolm laughed. "True enough. Must be a shifter thing because all the pups are like that."

Didn't she know it. "Thanks for cooking breakfast. This is a nice treat."

"This won't be the only morning it happens."

A shiver of awareness slid down her spine at his words. She certainly hoped not.

"Look," he said in an oddly careful tone as he set a plate piled high with far too much sausage, eggs and fruit in front of her. Though she *was* pretty hungry after last night so… maybe she could eat it all.

"This sounds like an ominous tone," she murmured, wondering if something had happened with the pack while she'd been asleep.

He sat next to her, his expression serious.

"You're not eating?" she asked when he didn't respond.

"Nah. I've been eating all morning."

She cut one of the sausage links with her fork, bracing herself for bad news. "Just spill it."

"I would like you to stay on the property today."

She frowned. "Why?"

"Because of the wolf we've spotted. I don't like the way the deaths escalated so quickly. If he's going feral, he'll try to go after shifters next."

Her first concern was protecting Elijah. "You think our pack is in danger?"

"Not technically. It just looks like a wolf has gone feral. But I want to be smart about it."

"Well, I plan to go to town today to meet up with Erica so the boys can have a play date. I'll be fine there." Especially if that wolf had gone feral. Because ferals tended to stay close to nature and away from densely populated human areas. They stayed where their wolf was most comfortable. In the forest. So it was fairly unlikely the wolf would make its way into town.

He rubbed the back of his head. "I would feel better if you stayed here."

He wasn't giving her an order, and she could appreciate safety measures, but something about his tone was bothering her. Mainly because it made more sense if she went to town. "Are you asking anyone else to stay on the property? Erica? My mom?"

He shifted in his seat, suddenly looking uncomfortable. And that's when she realized the answer was no.

"You're just asking *me* to stay put?"

"Yes."

She set her fork down, her stomach twisting into a tight ball. "Why?"

"Because I care about you and I want you close to me."

"No. You're telling me to stay put because you think I can't take care of myself."

"I didn't say that." He leaned forward, those blue eyes expressive.

"You didn't have to say that. I can read it in your expression. If you were truly worried, you would ask everybody to stay put. But you're just asking *me*."

"I'm just worried about you."

"No, you think I'm weak. How is that going to look to the rest of the pack?" His opinion of her stung.

He leaned back slightly, his frown growing. "No one's going to care."

"Maybe not now. But if you want me for your mate, an *alpha's mate*, you can't keep me under lock and key. I absolutely get that I'm not as physically strong as you, but you're trying to coddle me for no apparent reason. If anything, it makes more sense for me to be in town. You know how ferals are."

He nodded slowly but she could still see that he didn't like it.

"I lived with one man who told me where to go and how to live. I understand that's not what you're doing right now but you *are* treating me differently because of what I went through. You're treating me like I'm still a victim. The only reason I stayed so long is because of the danger to my mother. I don't think I deserve what happened to me. I'm not broken. And I'm not going to live my life in fear anytime some random threat happens to the pack. Because the others will notice and they'll never respect me as your mate. Sure, they'll still love me, but their wolf sides won't respect me. And that does both of us a disservice. Because eventually, it'll tear down everything you've fought to build here."

He scrubbed a hand over his face. But he didn't respond. Which just annoyed her.

Finally he cleared his throat. "You're right."

She blinked in surprise. She'd been gearing up for an argument, not... this.

Which earned a wry smile from him. "Don't look so shocked. I'm an alpha, but I can admit when I'm wrong."

"Well, that's good to know. Especially since I'm right most of the time." Her tart words were teasing.

He let out a startled laugh. "I agree with what you said. I wasn't looking at it from that perspective. However, I am sending an escort with you into town today."

She started to argue but he shook his head. "This has nothing to do with me not respecting you and everything to do with you being my future mate. I care about you, which means I get to act irrationally. Every single male wolf in this pack acts irrationally where their mate is concerned."

"How about every mated male wolf on the planet does," she murmured. "At least the good ones."

He gave her a half-smile as he nodded in agreement.

"Fine. That works for me." She could definitely live with an escort. She knew her strengths and weaknesses, but she wouldn't have him treat her with kid gloves. That would get old for both of them really fast. She wanted a partner, not a parent or a jailer.

"Is this our first disagreement?"

"I don't even think it was a disagreement," she murmured, glancing over at Elijah as he interrupted them with a loud shout of "Mama!" Oh yeah, he was definitely not getting the attention he wanted right now.

"Sit," Malcolm said when she started to get up. "Eat and enjoy. I've got this. He needs a bath anyway. I think he's covered in more food than he ate."

"Are you sure you're up to that?"

He gave her a dry look. "I've got two nephews. And I even know how to change dirty diapers."

She laughed lightly. "All right. Thank you for breakfast and… for listening."

Leaning down, he quickly kissed her with the same intensity from last night, and the knot in her belly eased. "You don't have to thank me for that."

* * *

"I have a feeling these guys are going to bring back far too much sand," Leslie said, stretching her legs out as she leaned back on the bench at the park.

Next to her, Erica snorted. "No kidding. I don't even care. This is just the perfect age where they still love and need you—and aren't talking back yet."

Nodding, Leslie picked up her water and took a sip as she watched Elijah attempt to dig into the sand at a local park that thankfully had no humans in it right now. If they showed up, Leslie and Erica and the boys would have to leave just in case their little ones decided to shift to wolf form.

So far they seemed to understand that they had to stay in human form but they were so young and didn't always comprehend the whys of things, even if they were more advanced than humans the same age.

Ursula—one of the pack's toughest warriors—had come as Leslie's "escort" and she was currently on the phone with someone a few feet away. Leslie had no doubt that if there was an emergency, the other woman would be prepared, but it was pretty clear she was dealing with pack business as well. All the warriors were busy trying to hunt down that feral wolf before it caused them more problems.

Leslie smiled when she saw her mom's familiar truck rumble into the parking lot. She'd let her mom know she'd be here, and she saw that a couple other female packmates had followed with another handful of pups.

"So pretty soon we're going to be sisters-in-law, huh?" Erica grinned at her, drawing her attention away from the parking lot.

It felt weird to agree but she nodded, even if she didn't say the words aloud.

"I get it, you don't want to jinx it. But Malcolm is over the moon for you. Has been for a long time."

"Well, I'm definitely over the moon for him." Last night had been incredible, and she'd realized that she was completely comfortable with him now. She'd been vulnerable with him in bed and he'd been nothing but giving. And his tongue? Oh, his wicked, wicked tongue. She shelved that thought so her mind didn't go wild and wayward but she was looking forward to seeing him when she got back this afternoon.

As far as she was concerned, she was ready to mate, ready to take everything he had to offer. After the way he'd been thoughtful this morning instead of trying to bully her into staying on the pack's land, she'd realized that all her fears were for nothing. Over the last year and a half, he'd shown her exactly who he was over and over, and she trusted in him. In them. They'd been building up to this, she just hadn't realized it until now.

"Oh, I know. The whole pack has been waiting for you guys to finally get together."

"Seriously?" She really had been living in a bubble.

"Yeah. There might even be a tiny bet going on as to when you guys would finally stop dancing around each other."

She blinked. "I don't know what to say to that."

"Well, you can say that you'll put him out of his misery and finally mate him tonight—and I'll win a couple hundred bucks."

Shaking her head in amusement, she looked back at the kids who were tumbling around in the sandbox and playing with the beach toys Erica had brought. It might not be the beach but the toys worked just as well here.

The boys started shouting with joy when the other kids arrived, crawling into the sandbox with them.

Elijah held out a toy to a new arrival, Ansley. They were about the same age, though she had a lot more hair than Elijah did. She immediately took the shovel and popped the handle in her mouth and started gnawing on it.

So maybe these kids weren't that much more advanced than humans.

At the sound of a nearby ice cream truck, one of the kids stood up and started toddling towards the edge of the sandbox, clearly on a mission.

Elijah just looked around because he had no idea what the ice cream truck sound was.

"I got this." Her mom swooped in and picked up Elijah before Leslie could even stand.

"Thanks, Mom, I've got some money."

Luna just waved her away as the other moms and packmates picked up the little ones.

Ursula grabbed the twins, so Erica stayed on the bench and grinned. "It's so nice to have packmates to help out. I can't imagine how hard it is for people without a support system. When would you ever sleep?"

"No kidding. It's hard enough *with* help. I can't imagine it without." Joining this pack had changed her and Elijah's lives for the better in every way.

The ice cream truck pulled into the gravel parking lot, that familiar music blaring away and bringing back a lot of memories from her own childhood. "I'm going to get something too. You want anything?" As she stood to join them, a somewhat familiar scent lingered in the air. She couldn't put her finger on it but something about it bothered her and it must have shown on her face.

"What is it?" Erica asked, standing next to her.

"I'm not sure." Muscles pulled taut, she hurried across the grassy area, over the sidewalk and onto the gravel parking lot with Erica right beside her.

As her mom reached the front of the line with Elijah, Leslie's heart rate increased as she looked around. It almost smelled like her dead mate. She knew for a fact that he was gone, but still, that scent lingered in the air. It wasn't him, but it had familiar undertones and it made her queasy.

She started to call out to her mom when the man behind the ice cream truck window leaned forward. She didn't know who he was, but the intent in his eyes was clear.

"No!" She screamed as he lunged at her mom and Elijah.

She raced forward, a surge of strength punching through her as she passed a metal bicycle rack. Without thinking, she ripped one of the metal loops free and ran full speed across the parking lot as her mom and all the others sprinted away with the kids in hand.

Holding tight to the metal pipe, she reared back and threw it with all her supernatural wolf strength. Even if there had been humans around, she wouldn't have cared.

The male dodged out of the way, falling back into the interior of the truck as the pipe shattered the passenger window.

He jumped back up, his eyes flashing to bright yellow.

Definitely wolf. She didn't recognize him even if his scent was familiar.

His fangs and claws extended and for a moment, she thought he was going to jump through the service window at her.

She took on her fighting stance, aware of Erica doing the same beside her.

Ursula raced passed them, having given the twins over to someone.

Whatever the male saw in her eyes, he turned and jumped into the front seat, his tires throwing up gravel as he raced away.

"Should we go after him?" Erica asked.

Leslie only wanted to hold Elijah close, and going after a strange wolf who'd wanted to take her kid? No, she needed to get him to the safety of the pack's land. She already had her phone out. "I'm calling Malcolm," Leslie said. "And we need to get all the kids back to pack property now. He looked as if he wanted to take Elijah. Or it could have been any one of the kids. That was crazy bold to do in the middle of the day. We'll all drive together. No one gets separated," she said as she took a now crying Elijah from her mom's arms and held the phone up to one ear.

He might not understand what had happened but he knew the energy in the air had shifted. As soon as she gathered him into her arms, he buried his face against her neck and started to settle down immediately. Her heart rate slowed, her son's sweet scent calming her.

Something about that wolf was familiar but she didn't know him, that much she was sure of. And they needed to figure out who he was and what he'd wanted. Immediately. She breathed out a sigh of relief as Malcolm answered.

"Hey, my sweet wolf." His deep, rumbly voice rolled over her like a soothing balm to all her frayed edges.

She blinked back the sudden prick of wetness in her eyes as she hurried with the others to their vehicles. "I'm so glad to hear your voice. We have an emergency."

CHAPTER THIRTEEN

"This is it," Malcolm said to Hudson as they neared the cabin about a mile off the highway.

The place bordered Kendrick territory but he didn't own the land it was on. A dilapidated barn-type structure sat next to an equally falling-down cabin with boarded-up windows and the stench of thick mold and dead rodents that even humans would be able to smell.

But that scent didn't cover up the scent of the wolf who'd tried to take Elijah.

Malcolm was alpha for a reason, and he'd tracked the guy here after meeting Ursula at the park. The male's rage had left a distinctive scent trail, making it easier to follow.

When he'd heard Leslie's steady, but worried voice telling him what had happened, he'd never been so panicked in his life. Hell, he didn't do panic. Until that moment. He'd wanted nothing more than to bundle up her and Elijah and protect them from the world.

"The ice cream truck is in the barn," Jared said as he slid back into place next to Hudson and Malcolm. He'd gone out as a scout to see what he could find.

"We don't kill him." Malcolm said quietly. Not yet anyway. He wanted answers first—though the male was soon going to die for trying to kidnap one of their pups.

Killing wolves and trespassing was bad, but hurting a pup? Trying to take a baby? There was no forgiveness for that. Not in the shifter world and not in the human world. Humans could be particularly savage as well when it came to protecting their children. That was something he appreciated about them.

"That's an order," he continued. "But if he provokes you, defend yourselves." He wanted to know why this guy was here and if he had backup, but the pack's safety came first. He didn't want anyone dying or getting hurt because of his order.

"Let's go draw him out," Malcolm said, stepping out of his hiding spot, the others following suit.

The thick line of trees surrounding the cabin protected them from being sighted but by now, it was possible the wolf inside had smelled them. Hell, more than possible. Probable.

Leslie said she wasn't sure what the guy had wanted other than to take Elijah or maybe one of the other kids. She said the look in his eyes had been clear and malicious and that his scent had been familiar, almost like her ex's. But her ex's parents, brothers and his entire former pack were dead. Even so, Malcolm trusted her instincts.

"Come and get me!" a voice from inside the cabin shouted.

"Let's do this." He raced forward as the others immediately dispersed, surrounding the cabin in a giant circle.

Malcolm grabbed his stun grenade and pulled the pin free. Normally he didn't favor using human weapons because they were far too messy, but he wanted to draw this guy out and deal with him immediately. And he wasn't risking that they walk into a trap.

"Go!" he shouted as he drew his arm back and threw the grenade at the cabin.

It crashed through one of the front windows just as he heard more glass breaking.

There was a vicious curse from inside, then a man dove out the front door as the cabin exploded. Fire and smoke billowed into the air as a man rolled across the dirt, finally stopping on all fours though he was in human form still.

"You can't outrun us." Voice low and savage, Malcolm stalked toward the man who'd jumped to his feet, his hands balled into fists.

Up close, he sensed the old power of the male rolling off him. This was a very old wolf, maybe four or five hundred years old. It wasn't a science but he could guess shifter age based on the emission of power.

"Who are you and what do you want?" Malcolm growled at him.

"I want what's rightfully mine. Elijah is my great-grandson. And I know that bitch got Jude killed."

Malcolm's wolf was in his eyes, his claws extending in an instant. But he reined himself in. Barely. "So you thought kidnapping a child from his mother in broad daylight on my territory was wise?"

"He's mine. He's all I have left of my family line!" The male growled, his face already starting to shift, his jaw elongating and fur sprouting all over his arms and hands. "A boy shouldn't be raised by a weak female. He's mine to raise. I'll do it right. And it's my right."

Without even asking, Malcolm understood why this male had killed those wolves on his property. He wasn't a feral; he'd been trying to force the pack to increase security on the property. Because if there was more security on the property, there would be less in town. This wolf couldn't have guaranteed that he'd catch Leslie in town, but it would be a whole lot easier if they had less security. At least that was Malcolm's guess.

He didn't care why the guy had done it, he just knew this wolf had to die. Because he would never stop coming after Leslie or Elijah. He would die trying to get what he wanted.

"Your grandson got what he deserved. He was a weak wolf who abused his own mate," he spat, unable to hide his disgust. That pathetic excuse for a male had hurt Leslie over and over.

The wolf's eyes flared. "So says the male who's fucking the bitch now. I can scent her all over you!"

Malcolm growled low in his throat and let the shift overcome him. There would be no more words. No talking. This wolf wanted a fight and he was going to get one. If the male had backup, they would have come out by now.

The other wolf shifted as well, snarling and growling and snapping at him as if he actually were a feral.

Malcolm knew where every single one of his sentries was, and if for some reason he failed, they would finish off this wolf. But he wasn't going to fail. Not when he had so much to fight for.

His wolves created a ring around them as they started to circle each other. As he eyed the wolf, he saw that it had many scars, his eyes glowing a bright, maniacal amber. The dwindling fire from the grenade blasts reflecting in them made him look even more unhinged.

Malcolm charged hard and fast, taking the first swipe. He went straight for the wolf's eyes, slashing down in a sharp arc as he attempted to blind him.

The male's head snapped to the left and he let out a snarl of pain even as he swiped back.

Malcolm bared his teeth, growling low in his throat. He wasn't going to drag this out, wasn't going to play with his prey. He needed this done quick and fast. He had to take the male's head off or his heart out. The head would be the easiest.

The wolf rushed at him now, jaws open wide. Malcolm snapped back, his teeth razor sharp as he went for the male's throat.

They clashed midair, battling, biting, slicing. Pain exploded in his underbelly but he didn't care.

He bit and sliced through skin and cartilage anywhere possible as he struggled to get the wolf down. Once he had the other wolf pinned on the ground, his jaws wrapped around his throat in an unforgiving grip.

Agony pierced through his side, shoulder and belly even as he bit down, tearing, tearing, then tossing the severed head away.

As the wolf's body collapsed into the dirt, blood spreading over the ground, Malcolm dropped beside him.

He dragged in ragged breaths, trying to take stock of his injuries—but everything hurt. He wanted to shift back, but had to stay in wolf form if he was going to heal.

He was vaguely aware of his brother in human form beside him, cursing up a storm as he lifted Malcolm into his arms with the help of another wolf. Damn, he must be worse off than he thought. He tried to move, but more pain rocketed through him.

"Let's get him back to the healer," Hudson said. "Call her and let her know we're on the way."

"Someone call Leslie," someone else said.

"I'll dispose of the body," Ursula said.

Malcolm tried to stay awake, tried to hold on to consciousness, but darkness started to take him under, creeping in and not letting go.

The only thing he was positive of was that the threat to Leslie and Elijah was gone. That was all he needed to know.

She was safe, and so was their son.

CHAPTER FOURTEEN

Leslie was aware of Malcolm waking up even though his eyes weren't open. His breathing had subtly changed, and since she had her head on his chest, she'd noticed it right away.

"How are you feeling?" She kept her voice low, not wanting to overwhelm him. He'd been asleep since his fight with her ex's grandfather.

All his wounds had healed and he'd shifted back to human form, but he'd been sleeping soundly the last two hours, his body needing to recharge. It didn't matter that he was an alpha, he wasn't invincible, and sleep was the only thing that helped. She hadn't left his side the entire time. She might not be his mate yet, but she'd basically invoked those rights and screw anyone who tried to get in her way. Not that anyone had.

"Did I imagine you yelling at everybody to get out of here?" he murmured in that deep, rumbly growl she loved.

"You did not imagine that. Your brother and our packmates were driving me crazy, so I might have shouted at all of them to leave so you could sleep."

He smiled and finally opened his eyes, a crystal-clear blue. "A true alpha's mate."

She smiled and cupped his cheek. "Just a scared one. I was so afraid of losing you," she whispered.

"I'm not going anywhere."

"No, you're not." She wouldn't let him.

"I love you," he blurted before she could say the exact same thing.

"You stole my line," she murmured. "I love you too. I realized it this morning when you didn't argue or try to go all alpha on me and insist that I stay home. Though in hindsight, maybe I should have."

"It wouldn't have mattered. He was coming for Elijah. If it hadn't been today, it would've been another day. He set the stage to make it look like a feral was on our property. It was very conniving."

Closing her eyes, she lay her head on his chest again. "I'd completely forgotten about him. Jude mentioned him a couple times but said he hadn't seen him in over fifty years. He mostly roamed and preferred staying in wolf form. He obviously heard about what happened to my former pack. I can't believe he tried to take Elijah."

"I can. Some wolves are just bad." He jolted upright suddenly. "Where's Elijah?"

"He's fine, silly man. I wouldn't be so calm with you right now if he wasn't. He's with my mom and a couple of the warriors and he has no clue what happened. You killed the wolf who wanted to take him."

"Yeah, of course." He rubbed a hand over his face. "I don't know what's wrong with me."

"You just got in a fight to the death and you're probably a little disoriented," she said dryly. "Nothing is wrong with you. Thank you for what you did. Though thank you is far too weak of a sentiment. I'll sleep easier now." She shuddered as she thought of that monster wanting to take her baby boy. If they hadn't caught him so quickly, she wouldn't have been able to rest until they had.

"You'll sleep every night in my bed," he ordered.

"That sounds pretty good to me." Did it ever. God, she didn't want to spend one night without this wonderful male. She didn't care that he was the alpha, she just cared that he was hers. For always.

He paused, watching her carefully. "You're going to move in with me?"

"I've already checked out your closet. I even started measuring to make sure you have enough space for all my stuff," she said teasingly. She hadn't looked in his closet, and she didn't have much stuff anyway, but she loved the way his mouth curved up at her teasing words. "How are you feeling, really?" she continued. She'd always thought of him as invincible but when they'd brought him in, covered in blood... she didn't think she'd ever get that sight out of her head. She'd washed away his blood after the healer had fixed him up and now he had no wounds at all. That was more than shifter healing and more than the healer's boost of energy—he'd healed so fast because he was an alpha. That hadn't alleviated her fear any. She hadn't felt whole until he'd opened his eyes.

"I feel like I could use a shower."

She popped up and held out a hand for him. "I can help with that."

He was already shirtless so he just stripped off his pants, making her blink in surprise. Okay, then.

She knew they were officially together and that she had all sorts of naked privileges with him, but it was still a shock that he was just stripping in front of her. A very nice shock.

"You need to get naked too," he said, reaching for the hem of her T-shirt.

And yeah, she really liked the sound of that. Soon he had it and her pants off and was walking her backward to the bathroom as he devoured her mouth with his.

Apparently getting almost killed wasn't slowing this wolf down at all. She barely felt the blast of water as he backed her up against the cool tile wall of the huge shower.

She arched up into him as he held her close, pinning her in place against the wall.

"I'm ready for everything," she murmured against his mouth. "I want you to claim me." They'd had so much damn foreplay the night before, and he had almost died.

Literally almost *died*.

She didn't want to wait another second to be fully claimed by him. She was glad that he didn't question her or ask if she was sure. She knew her own mind and he clearly agreed. It was definitely time.

He gently teased her breasts into rock-hard points as he continued kissing her. It was too much and not enough. She nearly begged for more but it was as if he read her mind, because one big hand strayed lower between their bodies and cupped her mound.

She loved the feel of him holding her so possessively. With her ex, he'd wanted to keep her locked up, to own her. Malcolm was protective and yes, possessive. But he just wanted her for who she was, and he saw her as an equal. The pull she felt to him was indescribable, and she knew that the mating pull was as real as the sun.

He was her true mate.

Water rushed all around them, creating a sort of barrier from the outside world as he slowly slid a finger inside her.

She rolled her hips against it, needing more. So much more. And she wasn't feeling patient. Not after knowing she could have lost him before they'd even had a chance at a future.

She reached between them and wrapped her fingers around his hard erection. She wanted him fully inside her, now.

Taking her cue, he shifted slightly, pressing his thick cock against her entrance. She moaned at just the feel of his head pushing inside her. He was so thick, and she felt so damn needy and desperate.

Her nipples were tightened into hard little buds and each time they rubbed against his chest, the friction drove her crazy. But not as crazy as when he thrust completely home, filling her.

She gasped as she took him completely in, needing a moment to get used to his size.

He remained still, nibbling little kisses along her neck and behind her ear, focusing on the sensitive spot he'd already figured out drove her crazy.

"You feel so good," she whispered, barely able to talk at all. This was everything she'd fantasized about, but so much better.

He simply growled against her neck, the vibration rolling through her in waves of heat.

She rolled her hips once even as she reached around and dug her fingers into his back, then down to his sculpted ass. She couldn't believe this male was all hers—and she wasn't letting go.

He growled against her skin again and she felt his canines raking against her neck.

She couldn't wait for him to mark her, to make her completely his. "Move, please." She didn't care if she was begging.

That was all the encouragement he needed. He started moving, his thick length dragging against her inner walls, and that alone nearly pushed her over the edge as he hit her G-spot over and over.

It was too much and not enough. "Faster," she demanded. The friction was almost enough to get her there, and after going out of her mind with worry, she needed this. He was safe and whole and while she knew that, she'd been scared for him.

"I like bossy Leslie," he murmured before capturing her mouth in a possessive claiming.

She couldn't even smile at his words as she arched her back into him. Because as they lost themselves in each other, she lost the ability to think. The only thing that mattered was pleasure and claiming each other as he thrust inside her over and over.

When he reached between their bodies and stroked her clit, she surged into orgasm, pleasure punching out to all her nerve endings as she seemed to climax forever.

As she reached her peak, he bit into her neck, his canines piercing her skin in a full claiming. Pleasure and pain mixed together as he climaxed, releasing himself inside her in long, hard strokes.

She'd never felt so whole in her life, so completely satisfied and wonderful as she did in that moment. She clung to him as the tremors of her orgasm finally subsided, and he held on to her just as tight. She never, ever wanted to let go.

"That was incredible," she murmured, kissing his neck as the hot water continued to beat down on them.

He drew back slightly, watching her closely. "I've wondered what my mate would be like for almost two-hundred years. You were definitely worth the wait."

Damn it, the man knew exactly what to say to make her cry. Tears sprung to her eyes but he kissed them away.

And she was very aware that he was growing hard inside her again. Thank you, shifter genes.

Energized and keyed up, she knew they weren't through. Not even close.

She planned to spend all night and all day in bed with this man who had completely stolen her heart.

It had taken some rough roads to get here, but he was worth the wait.

He was worth everything.

—THE END—

Thank you for reading Chosen Mate I really hope you enjoyed it. If you don't want to miss any future releases, please feel free to join my newsletter. Find the signup link on my website: https://www.katiereus.com

Wolf's Mate excerpt
Copyright © 2018 Katie Reus

Erica laid her head against Hudson's chest as she trailed her fingers up his rock-hard abs—and over his plethora of tattoos. Everything about him was muscular and defined, which was common among shifters, wolf or otherwise. But the tattoos? He was the first shifter she'd met who had so many. Most of them were linked to his original Scottish clan or pack related things. Luckily none of them were for any past lovers. Something she would never be okay with.

She knew her time with him was coming to an end, and though she wanted to stall even longer, she shouldn't. Not if she wanted to keep her heart in one piece. Mostly. Because it was cracking already at the thought of leaving him. Of leaving Montana.

"Keep touching me like that and I'm going to be inside you in another ten seconds," he murmured, his voice all rough and raspy, sending shivers down her spine.

The man just had to open that sexy mouth and she was mush. "You say that like it's a bad thing." The truth was it didn't matter if she was touching him, he couldn't seem to keep his hands off her. Something she very much appreciated. Because she liked orgasms. A lot.

"Stay another couple days," he murmured.

It was on the tip of her tongue to say yes. She desperately wanted to. One month with him wasn't enough.

But he hadn't offered her anything. He'd simply asked her 'to stay in Montana'. And while he might not be alpha of the Kendrick pack, he was second-in-command and terribly alpha in nature. Shifters like him went for what they wanted. If he wanted to claim her, for her to stay permanently, he would have asked for that. Simple as that. Because the male was over two hundred years old. He was being honest, she could give him that. He'd never promised her anything and she'd taken exactly what he'd been offering—a lot of fun.

So she might want him—and genuinely want more than just sex—but she wasn't going to throw herself at him. Hell no. She was going to walk away with her pride intact and head back to her own pack. Even if it carved her up inside to do so. Because sometime during the last month she'd fallen for him. Hard. It would have been impossible not to. He'd opened up about his past, brought her breakfast in bed—woke her up with oral sex almost every other morning—and was simply the sweetest man she'd ever met.

"We've been over this." She gently nipped at his bare chest. Damn she was going to miss him. For more reasons than the hard body underneath her.

"You're not on a schedule." He was dangerously close to pouting, which under any other circumstance, would have made her giggle.

But she didn't feel like laughing now. Not when the ache in her chest had settled in deep and wasn't letting up anytime soon.

She pushed up on the bed to look into those startling blue eyes. His dark hair was a little longer than most of his packmates, curling around his ears. "I might not be on a hard schedule, but I still need to get back. It's been a year. My pack needs me." After college she'd started working at one of the pack's salons. Then when the owner had up and mated—and moved—Erica had decided to reevaluate her own life.

So she'd taken a year to herself and roamed around the globe, mainly sticking to the United States. During the last month of her trip, she'd been traveling across Montana and had met the very sexy Hudson Kendrick. She'd never imagined meeting someone like him on her trip. All sexy, surly and incredibly giving in the bedroom—soooo giving. And everything about him was real and honest. What you saw with Hudson, you got.

In response, he simply growled at her, but there was no heat behind it. Not that it mattered, her wolf side knew on an intrinsic level that he would never actually hurt her so even his most terrifying growl didn't scare her. He started to say something when his phone buzzed.

Cursing, he snatched it off the bedside table and then cursed again when he looked at the screen. "It's my brother, we're having another issue on the border. I've got to take care of this."

Though she hated to do so, she rolled off him and let him get up. It was hard not to admire the view as he picked up his discarded jeans from the floor and tugged them on, covering all of that sexy bronze skin.

"I'm probably just going to head out while you're gone," she said carefully, watching him for his reaction.

He froze for a moment before turning to glare at her. "At least wait until I can take you to the airport."

She wanted to say yes but gave a noncommittal grunt. His brother, the alpha, had offered to fly her back to her home in Alabama on his private jet anytime she wanted. Apparently, there was a pilot currently on standby. Which was really nice, but also bad because she'd kept extending her stay for the last week. Because Hudson kept pushing for 'one more day'. Erica knew that if she waited for him to take her to the airport, she'd give him another day, and then another.

And then that whole pride thing? Yeah, she wasn't so sure she'd walk away with it intact. She'd do something stupid and then getting over him would be even harder. Try, impossible.

When Hudson's phone buzzed again, he did that sexy growling thing as he looked at it. More colorful curses followed before he tugged a long-sleeved T-shirt over his head. She stayed in bed, just watching him move, all lethal efficiency. Once he was dressed, with his boots on, he stalked toward the bed and leaned over her, placing both hands on either side of her head, effectively caging her in. Then he crushed his mouth to hers, a possessive claiming she felt all the way to her core.

Unfortunately, he didn't seem to want to claim her in reality. Because sex wasn't enough to keep her here. She wanted more than that. Something she hadn't realized until she'd met Hudson. The sex was great—better than great—but she needed more.

"I'll see you soon. Be naked when I get back."

Oh no, not responding to that. Nope. Because she wouldn't be here when he got back.

Once he was gone, she gave it five minutes before packing up her small bag and trying to ignore the spreading ache in her chest. She had to do this now. She hadn't brought much with her on her trip, because it was a whole lot easier to travel light. Now she was grateful for that. The sharpest sense of melancholy filtered through her as she hefted her bag and backpack up. It was time to go home.

So why did it feel like she was making the biggest mistake of her life by leaving? And why did it feel like she was leaving home instead?

KATIE'S COMPLETE BOOKLIST

Darkness Series
Darkness Awakened
Taste of Darkness
Beyond the Darkness
Hunted by Darkness
Into the Darkness
Saved by Darkness
Guardian of Darkness
Sentinel of Darkness
A Very Dragon Christmas
Darkness Rising

Deadly Ops Series
Targeted
Bound to Danger
Chasing Danger (novella)
Shattered Duty
Edge of Danger
A Covert Affair

Endgame Trilogy
Bishop's Knight
Bishop's Queen
Bishop's Endgame

Moon Shifter Series
Alpha Instinct
Lover's Instinct
Primal Possession
Mating Instinct
His Untamed Desire
Avenger's Heat
Hunter Reborn
Protective Instinct
Dark Protector
A Mate for Christmas

O'Connor Family Series
Merry Christmas, Baby
Tease Me, Baby
It's Me Again, Baby
Mistletoe Me, Baby

Red Stone Security Series
No One to Trust
Danger Next Door
Fatal Deception
Miami, Mistletoe & Murder
His to Protect
Breaking Her Rules
Protecting His Witness
Sinful Seduction
Under His Protection
Deadly Fallout
Sworn to Protect
Secret Obsession
Love Thy Enemy
Dangerous Protector
Lethal Game

Redemption Harbor Series
Resurrection
Savage Rising
Dangerous Witness
Innocent Target
Hunting Danger
Covert Games
Chasing Vengeance

Sin City Series (the Serafina)
First Surrender
Sensual Surrender
Sweetest Surrender
Dangerous Surrender

Verona Bay
Dark Memento

Linked books
Retribution
Tempting Danger

Non-series Romantic Suspense
Running From the Past
Dangerous Secrets
Killer Secrets
Deadly Obsession
Danger in Paradise
His Secret Past

Paranormal Romance
Destined Mate
Protector's Mate
A Jaguar's Kiss
Tempting the Jaguar
Enemy Mine
Heart of the Jaguar

SAVANNAH'S COMPLETE BOOKLIST

Contemporary Romance
Dangerous Deception
Everything to Lose
Adrianna's Cowboy
Tempting Alibi
Tempting Target
Tempting Trouble

Crescent Moon Series
Taming the Alpha
Claiming His Mate
Tempting His Mate
Saving His Mate
To Catch His Mate
Falling For His Mate
Wolf's Mate
Jaguar's Mate
Chosen Mate

Futuristic Romance
Heated Mating
Claiming Her Warriors
Claimed by the Warrior

Miami Scorcher Series
Unleashed Temptation
Worth the Risk
Power Unleashed
Dangerous Craving
Desire Unleashed

ABOUT THE AUTHOR

Katie Reus is the *New York Times* and *USA Today* bestselling author of the Red Stone Security series, the Darkness series and the Redemption Harbor series. She fell in love with romance at a young age thanks to books she pilfered from her mom's stash. Years later she loves reading romance almost as much as she loves writing it.

However, she didn't always know she wanted to be a writer. After changing majors many times, she finally graduated summa cum laude with a degree in psychology. Not long after that she discovered a new love. Writing. She now spends her days writing dark paranormal romance and sexy romantic suspense.

Made in United States
Orlando, FL
18 October 2024